MW01285818

Death Song

By JoAnn Conner

This book is dedicated to Tim and Tom,
and to all those who continue to fight evil,
even when the light is dim.

Other books by JoAnn Conner

Heartwood

"Heartwood is a fun little western written in simple language and straightforward sentence structure with a solid, if predictable, story line. Ms. Conner has done her research, so the basic historical facts are in place from which to spin her story of murder, survival, and love."
-Taylor Flynn, Tahoe Mountain News

This is an old-fashioned, cowboy/adventure/romance book that gets everything right. The setting is post Civil War Bridgeport, California in the Sierra Nevada Mountains. The plot is strong from the beginning and the pace is very satisfying.
-Mary E. Oney

Knowing this area really well, I loved this book! I wish it was longer or if there was a series made about the Bridgeport area. Well written and a quick read!
-K. Janowicz

Love Cowboy stories and love stories about California history. Wondrous read!
-Gary Stanton

The Mountain

Very enjoyable read. I like a good crime related story and this book had it. You have a witness to a crime nearly killed, but saved by the local Sheriff. Then they each dig in and their strong mindsets are at odds. The story flows easily and before you know it, it is over, but with a nice twist at the end.
-Terry Alexander

Couldn't put it down! Griping. Moves fast. Local info is fun. Surprises. Good story. Good drama. Flows well. Fun twists.
-Jim Biller

Chapter 1

Ginger nosed her Kia into the space for her apartment and sighed. She was hot and tired, and sat for a few minutes before pushing the driver door open and lifting her aching feet out. She groaned as her slender weight shifted to the high heels, which pinched her abused, slightly heat swollen, feet.

She was exhausted. She had performed two deliveries today; the first was a birthday party for children, where she showed up as a popular animated figure from a show geared to the primary age set. The plastic head she had to wear made it necessary to redo her makeup and touch up her hair before the second job. She really hated those plastic heads. They had to be wriggled over her own head and fit too snug around the neck for her taste. She always felt like there wasn't enough air inside those things, and with her slight claustrophobia, it reminded her of one of her bad asthma attacks.

She slipped her key into the lock and shoved her front door open, smiling as she thought of the second job. Dressed as a sexy waitress, she had been hired to deliver a singing birthday telegram to the hospital administrator as he sat in the cafeteria. The staff stood around the perimeter of the dining hall, laughing and clapping as she danced beside and around him, singing, and finally sat on the table in front of him, showing off a lot of shapely leg as she sang the grand finale. He was pleased, but embarrassed, as his staff cheered. It was fun, but now she just wanted to get out of these hot, tight clothes and relax in the coolness of her own little space.

"Home sweet home," she sighed as she stepped into her small apartment. Her brown eyes always went to the cross stitch of the saying and the space it held on her living room wall. The small, framed piece of fabric, colorfully stitched with love, was one of the few things she managed to salvage from her grandmother's home when she passed away. That was a memory that always brought a mixture of sadness and happy times to her thoughts.

Her grandmother had been such a loving, giving person who not only took Ginger in after her parents were killed in a plane crash, but she had also taken in dozens of foster children during the time Ginger was growing into a young woman. She still kept in contact with a few, who had become good friends as they grew up together. Several of the foster kids had come back for the funeral, and all gave credit to her grandmother for the life skills and love she had taught them during a dark part of their lives. In fact, Ginger had been surprised to find one of the young men had grown up and gone into the same line of work she had chosen.

She saw him for the first time in a decade, at the funeral. He had pulled her aside after the service and urged her not to tell anyone they shared a past. He was ashamed of being a foster child; he still harbored a smoldering anger towards his parents for breaking up their home. She had seen the venom in his eyes that day, and while she respected his demand, she did not understand.

She was shocked to find he worked at the same agency where she had just begun to work. She had not yet run into him at work, and he made it clear he wanted it kept on that level. When they did run into each other, they barely spoke, and never got together to remember the good times at her grandmother's house.

Ginger sighed and shook her head at the situation. She could not help him, so she had "let it go," as her grandmother used to say. She just put it out of her mind and focused on her job.

Ginger flipped the switch to turn on the sweet little lamp she had found in an antique store. The glass base and shade, with dangling amber colored beads, also reminded her of the grandmother that had raised her. It looked just like the one her grandmother had on her night stand for years until one of the foster kids got angry one day and shoved it to the floor, shattering it into a mass of broken glass.

The young girl was immediately crest fallen and tears brimmed from her eyes as she looked at the lamp and then at Ginger's grandmother, with real fear in her eyes. Her grandmother did not speak, but stepped forward, a pained look on her face as the girl threw up her arms to protect her face. Ginger would never forget how her grandmother had carefully taken the girl gently into a hug and spoke softly to her as she reassured her no one was going to hit her in their home. She told the child she was safe now. It was just a lamp and she understood Justine was going through a rough time. Ginger had taken her cue from her grandmother and had laid her hand on the girl's shoulder and told her she was there to help too. That was the beginning of a lifelong friendship.

Later, as her grandmother brushed Ginger's beautiful, thick, deep red hair before bed in one of the few special alone times they shared,

Ginger had asked her grandmother how come Justine had thrown up her arms to protect herself. In the mirror, she saw the sadness in the woman's face.

"Justine's mother gave birth to her when she was only sixteen. Her mother's parents threw her mother out of the house when they found out she was pregnant and the only one Justine's mother could turn to was the father of her baby.   The man her mother was with used to hit Justine and her mother until one day a teacher noticed the bruises on her arms when Justine got too warm playing tag and she took off her sweater." Her grandmother kissed her on top of her head.   "That is when Justine came to live with us," her grandmother continued. "Justine is very confused right now. Her mother is trying to get her back, but the court does not think that is a good idea. Justine wants to stay here with us, and with you." Her grandmother smiled. "She never had a friend before she met you." The woman sighed. "But, it is always hard to believe your mother or father might not be the people they should be. Justine just needs a lot of love right now." Ginger reflected on all the love her grandmother had managed to give to both her and the other kids that lived with them. Someday, she would like to be that kind of refuge for troubled kids, just like her grandmother had been.

Ginger and Justine became best friends and still kept in touch, but Justine had sent her regrets for the funeral. She was pregnant with her first child and on strict bed rest in a hospital. Her husband had come on the line and said after the baby was born and all was well, he would like to pay for a ticket for Ginger to come and visit. It had been a good reunion.

Ginger undid the clasp in her hair, shaking her locks free. She ran her hands through her thick, red hair, then rubbed her fingers quickly over her scalp in a refreshingly rapid massage. She reached behind her to unzip the tight dress, feeling the relief as the snug fabric loosened.

"I really need to talk to Chad about these costumes," she said to herself, taking a deep breath. Her asthma had been acting up, and between that and the pressure of the form fitting dress against her chest and rib cage, she felt like she couldn't take a full breath.

She kicked off the three inch heels, leaving them by the big easy chair in the living room, and walked bare foot to the kitchen. The coolness of the wood floor felt wonderful underneath her tired feet. She was glad the apartment had wood floors; it was actually one of the reasons she had chosen this apartment complex. Carpeted floors kept more dust in, which was not good for her asthma.

Ginger switched on another light and opened the refrigerator, reaching in for a cold diet cola. She popped the lid and took a long drink. She stood for a moment, looking at the contents of her refrigerator. She decided after her shower, she would settle for a dinner of cheese, crackers, and grapes, with some wine.

Ginger shut the refrigerator door, and turning towards the arch into the kitchen, froze, her eyes riveted to the back door. Her heart beat faster as she realized the door was open a crack. She took a deep breath and set her cola on the counter as she walked to the door.

"I'm such an idiot!" she chastised herself. "I could swear I locked the dead bolt on that this morning!" The door was old, and she loved the louvered window in the upper half. She had resisted having Jim, the manager, replace it because she liked the small, screened window, especially in the summer. But Jim had told her the frame was rotten and he needed to replace it because it would blow open if she didn't flip the dead bolt every time. He couldn't get another door that size with a window, so she had balked at getting it replaced. "I guess I'll have to get Jim in to replace it after all," she said, walking over to flip the dead bolt.

Ginger walked the few steps to her bedroom and stripped off her tight clothes. Slipping on her big, soft, peach colored bath robe, and sliding her feet into oversized, matching slippers, she padded into the bathroom. She shut the door out of habit, and wiggled the small bolt into place. Having been raised in a large family in a small house, where privacy was afforded only behind locked doors, it had become habit to lock the door behind her in the bathroom. The slip lock felt loose, and she made a mental note to grab a screw driver and tighten it up tomorrow.

Oh how she looked forward to these moments when she could slip into a hot shower and let the water pummel away the aches and worries of the day, undisturbed. *Best thing I ever bought was that shower massage head!* Ginger shed her robe and removed her make up, then reached in to turn on the shower. As she stepped into the shower, she realized something was terribly wrong. That smell! It couldn't be! This was all wrong, she had to stop it!

The building steam brought a strong smell of chlorine to her nostrils, which were already starting to burn. Her eyes stung as she frantically grasped the handles and turned to shut off the water, but the handles fell off the nubs. She couldn't stop the water pouring in! Her nostrils were burning and her throat was on fire! Ginger pounded on the wall, screaming for help and praying her neighbors would hear and send someone to stop the water.

She was gasping and choking now; she had to get fresh air! She pulled at the window, but it wouldn't budge. She tried frantically to dig her long nails into the seam between the window and the frame, but it did not move. She pounded on the glass, not caring if it broke, she needed to get good air into her lungs.

She had to get out of the room! Panic rose in her throat, and her brain seemed to reel with the realization that she could die! She stepped out of the tub enclosure and raced to the bathroom door, but the bolt was stuck and would not slide free. Suddenly, it fell off the door and she grabbed the handle of the door, only to find it turned uselessly in her hand. She tugged and pounded at the door, but it refused to come open.

Her inhaler! That would help! Terro struck her as she ripped open the medicine cabinet and grabbed her inhaler, hastily shaking the small tube and pressing the tab on the top, inhaling from the dispenser. Nothing came into her lungs! She shook it again and sucked in deep, but nothing came out of the canister.

Anxiety mounted as panic set in, and her reddened eyes darted around the small room, looking for anything that might be used to break the window. She could feel her chest beginning to tighten uncomfortably. She reached for the toilet brush and began banging on the thick, frosted window, jabbing the handle at the glass. If she could break it, she could get fresh air. The plastic handle broke, but the window did not. The frosted glass was thicker than normal window glass and she had nothing strong enough to break a hole for fresh air. Hysteria threatened to overtake her as ringing in her ears made her feel as if the room were closing in on her.

Ginger pounded with her fists, trying to scream for help as her throat closed. Black and gold spots blotted her vision as the pain in her chest grew. She felt herself falling and grabbed the shower curtain to try to break her fall. By the time she hit the side of the tub, she was unconscious.

Chapter 2

Frank Riley pulled his car onto the shoulder and shut off the engine. He pulled the keys out of the ignition and let his hand fall onto his knee, then slowly leaned forward and let his head rest on the steering wheel. The cold, hard circle felt good against his skin, and strangely soothed his headache. Closing his eyes, he sat for several minutes before he raised his head again, then slipped the keys into the pocket of his coat. *Would this day never end?*

He rubbed both hands over his face, feeling the stubble of a two day growth of beard. He ran his hands through his reddish brown hair, grabbing a handful on each side and holding it, as if he was trying to pull his brain awake through his scalp. He hadn't slept more than three hours in the past two days. And now, he had a new case. He would pay twenty bucks right now for a cup of really hot, strong coffee from Alpina Coffee Cafe, a popular favorite with the locals.

He drew in a deep breath and blew it out quickly as he opened the door and pulled his six foot three frame out of his Jeep Cherokee. Out of habit, he scanned the crowd that had gathered, then slowly began to walk up the slight incline into the parking lot. He picked his way through the squad cars, pulling his coat back to show the shield on his belt as uniforms turned to his approach.

The gray stone apartment building sat just off the main road through town, and was basically unremarkable, except for its clean appearance. It was one of the many privately owned small buildings of ten or so units, generally managed by a single handy man type or a couple that did the upkeep. More often than not, the manager was also the owner. Frank's experienced eye picked him out, standing just outside the open door guarded by a patrol officer.

The man was standing about ten feet from the open door of an apartment, staring straight ahead. Frank guessed him to be about forty, clad in navy blue sweats, and slender. His arms were crossed over his chest, and his head was moving slowly back and forth every few minutes. He did not notice Frank's approach

"Are you the manager?" Frank asked pleasantly. He looked at Frank with glazed, dark eyes, and shook his head slowly back and forth again, not really comprehending.

"Yeah," he replied flatly, returning his eyes to the open door of the end unit.

"I'm Detective Riley. What is your name?"

"Jim," he sighed heavily. "Jim Munson. I own and manage the building."

"Can you answer a few questions for me?" Frank asked, studying the man, who appeared to be in some kind of daze.

"What?" he asked, staring hard at Frank's badge. He shook his head briskly now and ran a bony hand over his face. He sighed. "Sure, what can I do for you, officer?"

"What can you tell me about the victim?"

"Ginger?" He shook his head back and forth again. "She was…" he bit his lower lip. "She was…everybody liked her," he said, moisture filling his eyes. "She was so nice to everybody. She was always checking on her neighbors, Carey and Thelma Clancy," he said, gesturing towards the front window of the apartment next to the end unit.

Frank turned to see an elderly couple sitting in the window, the man's arm around the shoulders of a tiny woman that must be Mrs. Clancy. He hadn't noticed them yet, as they sat in the dark, peering out at the scene in front of them.

"They have had some health problems this year, and have trouble getting around. Ginger would check in on them several times a week, offer to take them for groceries or pick up a prescription for them." He paused to wipe a tear from his eye. "It was the Clancy's who first called me about a problem. Their bathroom and Ginger's share the same wall." Jim glanced down at the pavement, then brought his eyes up again. "Poor Thelma was in the bathroom and heard pounding coming from Ginger's side of the wall. She came out and told Carey, and he went to Ginger's door. She didn't answer, so he went around to the back of the unit, where the bathroom window is, but by then the pounding had stopped. They were worried, so they called me."

"How long did it take you to get over here?" asked Frank.

"A few minutes," answered Jim. "I was just sitting down to read. The Clanceys don't ask for much, so I knew it had to be important for them to call after dark."

"Did you open the door to the apartment?" asked Frank. Jim nodded. "Did you go in?" Jim looked down at his shoes for a few minutes. When he looked back at Frank, his eyes were watery.

"Yeah," he said simply.

"Why don't you tell me what you saw," said Frank softly. He could see this was difficult for Jim.

"I knocked on the door, but no one answered." He blew out a breath. "So, I opened the door, and...I stepped back so fast I almost fell."The pain in his eyes was palpable. "The smell of chlorine was so strong." He licked his lips. "Then I...I remembered she was allergic to chlorine, so I had to go back in." Tears were streaming down his face now.

"Just take your time," said Frank, "in fact, why don't you sit down." Frank took his arm and led him to a bench on the walk between the apartments. Jim sank onto the bench and buried his face in his hands. Most people never saw even one dead body in their lives. He knew it was hard.

"I put my handkerchief over my mouth and ran in. I could hear the water still running." He was sobbing now. "The chlorine smell was so bad it was coming under the door! I tried to open the door, but it was stuck."

"The door was stuck?" asked Frank. "What do you mean?"

"It wouldn't open, I couldn't make the handle turn," he pulled a handkerchief out of his pocket and wiped his nose. So, I kicked it in," he rubbed his eyes, "and there she was, just lying in the tub. I grabbed her wrist and checked her pulse, but I knew she was..." Frank sat quietly as Jim slumped on the bench and brought his emotions under control. After a few minutes, Jim sat up and ran his hands over his face. He cleared his throat. "I'm sorry," he said, shaking his head.

"It's a normal reaction after finding someone in that condition," Frank said evenly.

"I couldn't even turn off the water!" he said. "I had to run back and grab a pair of channel locks to turn off the water. Even with the doors both open, the smell was so strong, I could hardly see to turn off the water." He dragged his sleeve over his eyes and looked at Frank.

Frank studied the man and then nodded to himself. He had more questions, but clearly, the man needed a few minutes to pull himself together. He gave Jim his card and wrote down Jim's number on a small notebook he carried in his breast pocket.

"I'm surprised the Clancy's are still up," said Jim, nodding towards their window. They go to bed pretty early, so they must be getting tired."

"Can you introduce us?" asked Frank, debating whether he

should talk to them tonight or wait. The body wasn't going anywhere, he decided, so probably good to at least talk to the Clancy's briefly.

"Sure," said Jim, turning towards the Clancy apartment. Frank followed him to the door, where Jim tapped softly. The door was opened a few inches and a tall, gaunt man of eighty peered out, shifting his eyes from Jim to Frank.

"Did you find out anything yet, Jim?" asked the old man. His face was drawn and had a grey cast to its sunken features.

"I don't know anything yet, Carey," said Jim, "but this is Detective Riley. Are you up for a few questions?" Carey turned his eyes to Frank and examined his face for a minute before he stepped back, swinging the door wide.

"Please, come in, Detective," he said. "I'm Carey Clancy and this is my wife, Thelma," he said, extending his hand. Frank shook his hand and nodded at Mrs. Clancy. Her face was very pale, but she offered him a weak smile of greeting.

"I'm sorry to intrude so late," Frank apologized. "I was hoping to get the story straight from you while it is still fresh in your mind."

"Yes, of course. I'm not sure we could go to sleep yet anyway," he said, shooting his wife a glance.

"Can you tell me what happened, as much as you know?" asked Frank. Carey looked at Thelma.

"I was brushing my teeth in the bathroom," said Thelma, "When I heard the water go on in Ginger's apartment. Our showers share the same pipes, so we sometimes hear each other," she explained. Frank looked at Jim, who was nodding his head. "It wasn't but a few minutes later that I heard pounding and I thought I heard a scream." Her voice broke and she looked at her husband, twisting her hands together.

"She came out of the bathroom, white as a sheet," added Carey. "I stepped in and heard pounding too, so I went outside and knocked on Ginger's door." He exchanged a painful look with his wife. "She didn't answer, so I went around to the back door, which sometimes isn't bolted and you can push it open."

"Why does it push open," asked Frank, shifting his gaze to Jim.

He looked at Frank. "The door is old and she wouldn't let me replace it. It didn't always latch right if you didn't turn the bolt. We all told Ginger to keep that door bolted. Even if she didn't believe there are people that might hurt her, we told her a bear could surprise her one night and she could get hurt." The Clanceys nodded in silent agreement.

"Was it bolted?" asked Frank.

"Yes, this time it was, so I went to her bathroom window, but it is frosted dual pane, so I couldn't hear or see anything." He looked at Frank with sadness in his eyes.

"That's when we called Jim," said Thelma. They all looked at Frank.

"Did you still hear the pounding when you went around to the window?" asked Frank.

"No," answered Carey. He walked over and sat down next to his wife, putting his arm around her shoulders. She leaned into him and cried softly.

"We were too late," said Jim, barely above a whisper. The atmosphere in the room was heavy with sorrow. These people obviously had great affection for the victim.

He gave the Clancy's his card and wrote down their phone number. "If you think of anything else, no matter how insignificant it may seem, please call me," he said.

"Yes, sir," said Carey.

"Please," said Thelma, hesitating before she raised pleading eyes to his, "please, find out what happened to that sweet girl." Tears ran down her cheeks.

"I'll be in touch," Frank said, and walked outside, leaving the three of them to comfort each other. He needed to get a look at the crime scene.

Chapter 3

Frank stood outside for a few minutes, inhaling deeply. The fresh air was invigorating, but he still wished for a cigarette and a cup of strong coffee. It had been six weeks since he quit smoking. Times like this were tough, and old habits hard to break.

He turned towards the open door on the ground floor. The young officer standing guard nodded, quickly acknowledging the shield Frank automatically thrust in his direction as he lifted the tape. He checked the young face as he walked by and shook his head. Were they just getting that much younger or was he getting that much older?

Stepping into the small apartment, he routinely scanned the room for first impressions. It was simply furnished with an overstuffed, forest green love seat and a matching, large, cozy chair. The end tables were dust free and uncluttered, as were the rest of the surfaces in the small apartment. Ginger was tidy.

"What have we got?" he asked the uniform standing in the hall outside the bathroom door.

"One victim, female, deceased. Appears to be about mid twenties," answered Foster. "Looks like she got a large dose of chlorine somehow," the young officer offered. He cleared his throat and flushed bright red when he met Frank's steady, immovable gaze. "I was first on the scene; responding to neighbors who heard pounding on the wall and screaming," he stated, all business now. "The manager opened the door and couldn't even go in right away because the chlorine was so strong it made his eyes burn."

Frank grunted an acknowledgement as he finally took his steel blue eyes off the rookie. This matched what Jim and the Clancy's had told him. Frank stepped to the open bathroom door. He noted the door hung on one hinge. He surveyed the bathroom and victim from the doorway, letting first impressions set themselves in his mind. His eyes moved to the young woman, still reclined in the tub. The shower curtain partially covered her; it must have fallen on her as she grabbed it, apparently trying to get out of the tub.

Carefully, he studied the room, noting every detail as he slowly scanned the scene. There were puddles on the floor, leading from the tub to the door and back again, it seemed. There were specks of blood on the window. He looked down at her hand splayed over the rim of the tub.

The manicured finger nails were broken and her hands were bloody. The Medical Examiner's bag was open on the floor next to the tub.

"Where's the ME?" he asked. He hadn't seen Jack in weeks, and he felt relief knowing he would be on the job.

"Right here," came a voice from behind him. He turned in surprise at the female voice. "Mind?" she said, looking at him and stepping deliberately between him and the corpse. Snapping gloves on and opening her bag, she started the automatic process of taking the body temperature and gathering tissue samples. The photographer snapped the pictures under her direction, getting the angles she would need later to finish her findings.

Frank stepped back and logged her every move from the doorway. Her dark hair fell in a soft wave to her shoulders, accentuating a creamy complexion. She was slim and moved with the ease of someone who was athletic. She was new, and she was pretty, he noted, but more importantly, was she any good? Would she miss something important? Not on his watch. Scrutinizing every step, he wondered why Jack Hogan was not here. Jack never missed an unusual case.

"Where's Jack?" he finally asked.

"Retired," she answered, without even looking in his direction.

"He can't be, he didn't tell me..." sputtered Frank. When had he last seen or talked to Jack? The old ME had been talking about retirement and exotic beaches for years, so long in fact, everyone had started to just nod and move the conversation along.

"He didn't need your permission," she commented, still not looking at him. Frank felt the heat rise up his neck to his face. Choking it down, he took a deep breath. He needed cooperation from the medical examiner in order to solve most of his cases.

"We got off to a bad start," he offered. "I'm Detective Frank Riley," he said, sounding lighter than he felt.

"Yeah, I figured that out," she murmured, carefully taking a tissue sample from the victim.

"And you are?" Frank fought to control his Scottish Irish temper.

"The new ME," she said absently, as she used a syringe to draw a sample of the water in the tub.

"Do you have a name?" Frank spat, irritated at the dismissive attitude.

"Doctor Sierra O'Malley," she replied, emphasizing the word doctor. She looked up at him for the first time. Her piercing green eyes seemed to regard him as an annoyance that was interfering with her work. She snapped her case shut, and nodded to the mortician's assistant as he appeared beside Frank in the doorway. The young man turned to leave.

"People don't always die of exposure to high doses of chlorine. What else did you find?" he asked. Sierra shot him a look of impatience.

"We'll let you know when we are done with the autopsy," she said, moving past him and out the door to the side of the apartment. "In here," she directed the coroner's gurney, "she's in the tub."

"Wait!" protested Frank, "I haven't had a chance to survey the scene! I just got here!"

"Should have been here sooner then," said the ME, defiantly looking him in the eyes. "I've already been here over an hour."

"But, I didn't even see the ME van when I pulled up!" he protested.

"Not that I have to justify anything to you, but we parked by the back door. Easier to get the body in and out without the crowds," she asserted, hands on her hips.

"Ready, doctor?"interrupted a voice from the door. Frank turned to see the young man with a gurney, and another holding a body bag.

"Take her," she directed the assistants from the mortuary.

"But I...!" Frank sputtered.

"You're going to want to get out of the way, Detective," she said, leveling a challenging look in his direction.

Frank fumed as he stepped back into the hall and watched them come in the room and prepare to take the body away. He backed up against the wall, still trying to catalog details in his mind. He glared in frustration at Sierra as she turned and walked out the door. Damn it, he needed answers!

Chapter 4

Frank parked his unmarked car in the lot in front of the building that bore the sign Medical Examiner. Conveniently located next to the police station, Frank had worn a path between the two buildings over the last twenty years on the job. He gazed at the gray stone building that sat recessed between the court house and the station. He reminisced about the numerous late night conversations he had held with the former ME, and he wondered how Doctor Jack Hogan had retired without a party, or at least a farewell luncheon. How had he missed such an important milestone?

His thoughts turned to the new Medical Examiner. He had heard nothing about her, and he needed her to be competent. He got out of the car and walked into the station, deciding he would do some investigation of his own before meeting with her again.

He used his department resources to delve into the employee files of the city. Every employee had to have a background check, so at this point, he was not breaking the rules – stretching them maybe, but not quite crossing the line.

Doctor Sierra O'Malley came to the City of South Lake Tahoe from Santa Cruz, California. She had a Bachelors degree from the University of San Francisco, Doctor of Medicine from Harvard, then Doctor of Pathology and Forensic Medicine from Stanford.

That was interesting. If she was already at Harvard, the best in the country for her field, why did she leave Harvard and come all the way across the country to Stanford for her study of Forensic medicine? Somehow, he did not see her as wanting anything less than number one.

"Wait a minute, what's this?" he peered at the screen for a minute, then hit the back cursor to check a date. There was a gap in her education. Two years. Why would she take two years off, then switch schools? He leaned back in his chair and stared at the screen in front of him. Suddenly, he laughed. "Nosy bugger, aren't you?" he said to himself as he switched off the screen. What did it matter anyway?

Frank shut down his computer and got up to get a cup of coffee, planning to review his notes one more time before heading home. The thick black fluid tasted burned, and he wrinkled his nose. He should stay and work through his thoughts on the case, but he was so tired, he couldn't think clearly. Several sips later, he tossed the paper cup in the garbage, grabbed his jacket, and walked out the door. He couldn't think straight anymore; he had to get some sleep.

Back in his car and settled behind the wheel, he turned the ignition and started to pull out of the space when movement caught his eye. It was Sierra O'Malley. She was walking slowly, as if she was too tired to move. Her arms were crossed in front of her, and she was looking down. Frank saw her wipe at her eyes, like she was crying. *What was going on?*

He continued to watch as she unlocked her car and got in. He waited until she drove away. There was something going on with Sierra O'Malley and he was going to make sure it didn't interfere with his case. He needed to find out more about her, but right now, sleep was a priority.

Chapter 5

Frank became aware of the sounds around him before he opened his eyes. Nothing unusual registered, and the bed felt so good. He liked his bed, with its warm, cozy down comforter, and he lay, hoping he could go back to sleep. He knew better. He opened his eyes and threw back the covers, rolling to a sitting position. Well, a few hours was better than none. Shoving his feet into the flip flops he kept by the bed, he padded out to the kitchen in his tee shirt and boxer shorts.

He hit the button on the side of the small coffee pot, opened the cupboard above the pot and reached for his travel mug. It wasn't there. Did he bring it in out of the car last night? He walked across the small kitchen to the door to the garage. Stepping through, he reached into the car and took his mug out of the cup holder. Back at the coffee pot, he realized it was surprisingly light. He set the pot back on the heat plate and sighed. He had been too tired last night to perform his habitual bedtime routine of preparing the coffee pot before he went to bed.

Frank made sure the coffee was actually brewing before heading to the bathroom. He showered and dressed quickly, filled a travel mug with his first coffee of the day, and proceeded out the door.

"At least I know my first cup will be fresh," he sighed. He crossed town easily, since it was well past rush hour. Frank pulled into a space between the Medical Examiner's office and the Police Department. He got out and began to walk towards the department, when he suddenly decided to go to the ME office first. He needed answers to move his investigation forward.

"Hey Frank! Good to see you!" said Bruce Trujillo, as Frank pushed through the doors and walked up to the first desk. He gave the assistant ME a big grin.

"Hey yourself, Bruce, how have you been?" Frank replied as they clapped each other on the shoulders. Frank met Bruce two years ago when they worked a case together. Ten years younger than Frank, the two men had developed a mutual respect when they each showed dedication and a determination to search for the answers until the case was solved. Bruce was very sharp, and detail oriented, a quality Frank always appreciated in their line of work.

"Keeping busy at work and play!" laughed Bruce. "How have you been?"

"You are looking fit! Still swim every day before work?" asked Frank.

"You bet!" replied Bruce. "The exercise helps keep my blood pressure down! Working here can be tough some days!"He grinned at Frank. "Still getting in a five mile run a couple of times a week?"

"Most weeks," Frank smiled back, patting his waistline. "I have to hold the line! It's in my genes to be a good runner; I wouldn't want to let my ancestral name sake down!" Both men laughed as Frank took a seat. "Besides, the bad guys are getting younger; I have to keep up!" Bruce nodded and offered Frank a Circus Peanut from the jar on his desk. Both men took one and popped it in their mouth.

What brings you here?" asked Bruce, chewing.

"Lookin' for the new ME."

"You and a dozen other single cops over there," he said, hooking a thumb towards the PD and grinning.

"Oh no," said Frank, shaking his head and putting both hands up, as if to ward off a blow. "I am absolutely not interested in Ms. O'Malley outside of work!" Bruce raised an eyebrow. "I just need to talk to her about a case that broke last night."

"Oh. Well, I just got back from four days off, so I haven't caught up yet," said Bruce. "One of my wife's cousins got married down in Morro Bay. It's a different kind of beautiful than we have here, but it is breath taking just the same."

"That's the second cousin this year to get married," laughed Frank. "How many more do you have?"

"Well, actually, Cecelia has a really cute cousin about your age. Smart, owns her own business…" he grinned at Frank.

"Negative," laughed Frank. "No offense to Cecelia or her cousin, but I think once is enough for me!"

"Uh huh," said Bruce, turning his attention to a white board with names on it, then shifting his gaze back to Frank. "I tried, just remember, when you are old and grey and decrepit!" He smirked as he looked back at the board, then at Frank. "O'Malley is down in the lab."

"Thanks, Bruce," said Frank, as he started to follow the familiar hallway down to the morgue and lab. He stopped and turned back to Bruce. "Hey, what happened with Jack, anyway? It's been several weeks since I was over here, but it sure seems like his retirement happened really fast."

"Yeah," said Bruce, looking down at the floor. "He just decided one day he was done." Frank's eyes sharpened as he noted Bruce avoided looking at him.

"Bruce," said Frank, "what's going on? Why did Jack leave so quickly?" Bruce put down the file he was holding and met Frank's stare.

"You should go by and see Jack," said Bruce. "That's all I can say." He looked down at the file again. "Sorry, Frank, I need to get this file to Rudy down the hall. See you later!" Bruce shot Frank a weak smile as he hurried down the hall in the opposite direction.

Frank stood in place for a few more minutes, his eyes following Bruce down the hall. Bruce looked back in his direction and hesitated a second, met Frank's eyes, then shook his head and went through the door to Rudy's office.

Was he getting paranoid, or was something off here? Frank's cop instinct was on high alert. He stood, for a few more minutes, gazing down the empty hall. Then, he turned and moved in the opposite direction towards the lab and morgue. He really needed to start getting more sleep.

Chapter 6

Frank pushed through the door into the stairwell and quickly descended to the basement. He could have taken the elevator, but he hated those things; too boxed in. He opened the door to the main downstairs hallway and walked to the big, stainless steel double metal doors. Heavy was the heartbreak that brought people through those weighted doors. He stood for a second, and looked through the window in the door.

Sierra O'Malley was standing over the metal autopsy table, facing the door, but intent on the body lying before her. Her hair was pulled back and clipped behind her neck, exposing a smooth, white neck, circled by a pair of small headphones, from which he could hear rock and roll music. Her lab coat was buttoned this morning, and she wore a plastic apron over it as well. He observed, with interest, how her hands moved gracefully, but expertly as she probed the lung on which she was focused.

The door yielded to the pressure of his hand as he entered the room. When he was only four feet from the table, she caught movement and jumped back a step in surprise before she recognized him.

"Detective," she said, pushing a button on the small headset and halting the music. "Nice of you to make it in before I go to lunch." Her green eyes drilled into him, then looked back down at Ginger's lung. He looked at his watch, noting the late start had made it almost eleven o'clock by the time he reached the lab. The color was rising up his neck as he looked back at her.

"I've been working a lot of twenty-four hour shifts!" he protested." She ignored him, examining the corpse as if he weren't even there. "I hadn't slept in two days when I went home last night." She was staring at him now. Damn it, why was he explaining himself to her? He thought he saw her eyes crinkle in a smile for a minute; she was laughing at him! "Who do you…" he began.

"Did you get my message?" she interrupted. He gave her a blank look and she rolled her eyes. "I left you a message two hours ago."

He blew out air and looked up at the ceiling. Frustrated at her curt remark, he pinched the bridge of his nose for a moment, then looked at her.

"Look," he said with his best smile, "we got off to a bad start."

He couldn't see anything but her eyes above the face mask, and they told him nothing. "I'm sorry." He wasn't sure what he was sorry for, but he just wanted them to have a smooth working relationship, so he gave a little. She glanced back down at the lung, then up at him.

"Did you find something?" he asked hopefully, detecting something in her expression.

She stripped off her gloves and walked over to put them and the mask in the trash receptacle. Coming back to face him, she picked up a clean scalpel and touched an area of the lung.

"See that?" she asked, meeting his eyes.

"What am I looking at?" he asked.

"See where the lungs attach to the bronchi tubes?" He nodded. "They are constricted!" Sierra waited for his reaction.

"Wouldn't that be normal if she was exposed to a substance, as in the chlorine, to which she might be allergic?" Frank didn't quite understand yet.

"Yes, but I saw one of your men bag an adrenergic bronchodilator he picked up off the floor in that bathroom," she continued.

"A what now?" He felt like this should make more sense than it did.

"An inhaler!" Her eyes were sparkling now. "Don't you see? If the inhaler were on the floor, she probably used it."

"Yeah," he answered, still at a loss.

"If she used the inhaler, she might have had a better chance. But look here," she said, pointing with the scalpel to a tube that was nearly closed completely.

"It should have opened her breathing passages at least a little," he said, realization dawning.

"Exactly!" she smiled. "I think if you check that inhaler you will find it empty."

"Why would she have an empty inhaler?" he puzzled.

"Maybe," said Sierra, "because someone really wanted her dead." The air was heavy with the weight of their thoughts as they stood frozen in place.

"I've got work to do," said Frank suddenly, as he strode rapidly to the door. He yanked it open and then stopped half way through. "Thanks Doc," he said, for which he got a smile.

Chapter 7

The sign on the door said "We Do It Your Way" with a list of services underneath. Frank cocked an eyebrow as he read the corny slogan. Singing Telegrams was third on the list, under Unique Birthday Parties, Bachelor and Bachelorette Parties, and above Themed Birthday Parties for Children, Specialty Flower Delivery, and Retirement Parties.

Frank walked through the door into a large room with a desk a few feet from the door. Behind the desk sat a young woman in a nurse's uniform that strained the buttons across the low cut top of the uniform. A nurse's hat perched on the top of her head, secured to her blond curls with bobby pins. Frank couldn't honestly remember the last time he actually saw a nurse wear such a hat, nor could he remember any woman he knew who used bobby pins.

Behind her were two other, larger desks, several file cabinets, and four racks of costumes. An attractive woman in a very short French Maid outfit, complete with black fish net stockings and three inch stiletto heels, was standing in front of the second desk, where a man in a cowboy shirt was sitting. Her arms were crossed and the cowboy was making gestures of appeasement.

"May I help you, Sir?" asked the nurse, flashing him a smile that looked even whiter framed in the bright red of her lipstick. Frank pulled his jacket back, revealing the badge on his belt. She stared at it for a moment, then brought large blue eyes up to meet his. He glanced at her name tag and had to choke back a laugh.

"Detective Frank Riley," he said to the receptionist. "Nurse, ahh, 'Ratchet'," I need to speak to the owner or manager please." He smiled his best smile, but it was more to keep himself from bursting out laughing than to win her cooperation. She twisted around and looked behind her.

" Just a minute, please," she said sweetly, very unlike the Nurse Ratchet character in "One Flew Over the Cuckoo's Nest." She stood to reveal a well sculpted pair of legs, clad in white stockings, secured by a garter belt, which just showed beneath the hem of her white mini skirt. He watched the sway of her slender hips as she walked over to the cowboy at the desk.

She gently touched his arm, then said something and the man

shot Frank an intense stare before coming around the desk to put his hand on the arm of the French maid. He spoke to the maid and she threw up her hands, then stomped in Frank's direction.

"I mean it, Chad, control your wife or I am out of here!" she snarled over her shoulder at the cowboy. The maid was almost to the door when it opened, and a well built man dressed as a firefighter entered in turnouts, with the top buttons on his pants undone and his jacket hanging open to reveal a strongly muscled torso.

"Hey, Michelle," the firefighter smiled at the French Maid as he held the door for her. He touched his hand to his helmet in a salute to the maid.

"Whatever, Ken," she snapped, as she went through the door. He stood watching her for a minute as she stormed down the sidewalk towards her car. "I could run this business better than either one of them," she threw back over her shoulder. His face was impassive as he walked towards Nurse Ratchet.

"Problems with personnel?" asked Frank, raising an eyebrow at Nurse Ratchet. The firefighter walked up to the desk.

"She's just having a bad day," the receptionist said absently, watching the other woman storm out the door. "Hey Ken," smiled the nurse, reaching for her water bottle," would you mind filling this for me?" She extended the water bottle to the man dressed as a fire fighter.

"Sure," he smiled, holding her eyes for a minute longer than necessary before walking over to the cooler with the bottle.

"Everybody has a bad day once in awhile," shrugged the nurse. Frank wasn't convinced. The firefighter returned with the water bottle and set it down on the desk with a smile for the nurse. "Thank you, Ken," she winked.

"Any assignments for me?" he asked the nurse, shooting Frank a quick, appraising glance.

"No, I'm sorry, Ken, "said the nurse, sounding sincere. "No bachelorette parties this week, I'm afraid."

He thumped a fist on the desk and frowned. "I'm outta here then," he said, as he turned towards an area marked dressing rooms.

"Detective Riley? You wanted to see me?" Frank turned to see the cowboy standing in front of him. "Chad Roberts; I'm the owner." He stuck out his hand and Frank shook it.

"Is there somewhere we can talk in private, Mr. Roberts?"

"Uh, sure, follow me please. Stephanie," he said to the nurse character, "the break room is closed right now - and hold my calls."

"Sure Chad," replied Stephanie, nodding her blond curls. Frank couldn't help but hold his breath, wondering if her nurse's hat would fall off her head.

Chad led the way down a short hallway to a very small room with a mini fridge, a microwave, and a coffee maker on the counter. A bistro style small table and two chairs were the only furniture in the room. Chad motioned to the coffee maker and raised an eyebrow at Frank, who nodded in assent. He took two cups out of the cupboard above the coffee maker, and poured. He opened the refrigerator and took out a small bottle of creamer, which he also held up in Frank's direction with a questioning look.

"A little, please," Frank spoke, noting that Chad was not overly inclined to be chatty.

"What's this all about, Detective," Chad finally spoke as he placed the two cups on the small table and took a seat, gesturing Frank to the other chair. *Wonder if this guy does mimes for the business*, Frank thought. More actions than speech.

"Do you have an employee named Ginger Snapper?" he asked, studying Chad carefully for a reaction. Chad smiled.

"Great stage name, huh? Her parents thought they were being funny. She would get irritated once in awhile, but with that red hair, she kinda had to expect it. I asked her once why she didn't change her name, but she didn't think it was funny, so I never brought it up again." He looked at Frank, expectantly.

"So, she did work for you," asked Frank, emphasizing that he hadn't actually answered the question.

"Oh, yeah, sure, one of our most popular employees, as a matter of fact." he nodded. Frank did not miss the use of the word "our."

"What did she do for your business?"

"Just about everything – she was very versatile. She could sing, dance, didn't mind working the bachelor parties…not a big fan of the kids parties though. Why, is she in trouble?"

"You said 'we' a minute ago, do you have a partner?" Frank asked, avoiding the question Chad posed.

"Yeah, my wife, Nina." He looked at Frank with a question in his eyes. "Should I get her?" he asked.

"No, not yet, I'd rather talk to you first," Frank replied. Chad sat back, concern blossoming on his face.

"Do I need an attorney?" he asked, more formality in his voice.

"Why, do you think you might need one?" asked Frank, looking steadily into his face. Chad started drumming his fingers on the table.

"No, I mean, I don't know! What is this all about?" he demanded.

"Ginger is dead." Chad looked as if he had been struck. His mouth hung open and his eyes were wide.

"That can't be! I mean, she was here yesterday! How? What happened?"

"We don't know yet, except it would appear there was a lot of chlorine involved."

"Chlorine?" Chad repeated. "No, that can't be right. Ginger was highly allergic to chlorine! She wouldn't do any pool parties because she was afraid to get near it. Hell, she wouldn't even rent an apartment in a place that had a pool!" He looked pale. "How did it happen?"

"What else can you tell me about her? Any next of kin?" asked Frank, deliberately not answering Chad's question.

"No," Chad murmured, "her parents died in a plane crash when she was really young. Her grandmother raised her with a bunch of foster kids, but her grandmother passed away several years ago."

"Anything else?" probed Frank.

"I..." started Chad, then stopped and ran his hand over his face. "Everybody liked her. She always remembered everyone's birthday," he said sadly.

"Did she have any other health issues or allergies?" asked Riley. Chad stared at him, then shook himself.

"Yeah," he paused, as if lost in thought. "Yeah, she had asthma. Always carried her inhaler in case she got around a trigger, you know?'

"What kind of trigger?"

"Like heavy perfume, pollen, even cigarette smoke sometimes. Definitely chlorine." He shook his head again. "I can't believe it. She just brought me a birthday cake two days ago."

Stomping feet echoed down the hallway and suddenly the door way was filled with a large woman of close to sixty years. She had huge hips and stood with her feet planted in bright red heels with bows on the back.

"Hooker shoes," Frank murmured, not realizing he had spoken aloud until Chad shot him a quizzical glance.

"We have work to do and you are sitting back here taking your damn sweet time on a break?" the woman fumed. Her hair was unkempt, and Frank wondered when she last brushed the dark roots with the red tips. "Who are you?" she demanded, swiveling her withering gaze in Frank's direction.

Frank stood, more out of courtesy and habit than respect, and pulled out his badge.

"Detective Frank Riley, M'am," he said, "and you are?" he asked, leveling a steady stare in her direction. His question brought a disgusted look to the woman's face, making her even more unattractive. It wasn't that she didn't have decent features, he mused, it was the meanness that seemed to ooze out of her.

"I'm Nina, the owner of this business!" she snapped. Frank glanced at Chad, who seemed more weary than afraid.

"This is my wife, and partner in the business," Chad offered, gesturing towards the woman in the doorway.

"I do most of the work around here!" she glared at Chad. "What do you want? She demanded, shifting her fiery stare to Frank. "We are busy!" she snapped, shooting Chad a murderous look.

"I'm here to ask some questions about Ginger Snapper," said Frank.

"That whore! What did she do, get arrested for moonlighting on the corner?" snarled Nina, twisting her red lips in a decidedly unattractive fashion. Frank studied her for a moment and decided she would be a vicious adversary if crossed. The caution signs went up in his brain.

"Nina!" said Chad. "What an awful thing to say! Ginger was one of our best employees!" said Chad, standing to face his wife.

"Well, I would expect you to take the side of your little pet!" said Nina, daggers flying out of her eyes. "The way she cooed over you and the other men around here, I'm sure she made you feel real special." She spat the last words at him, leaning forward and shaking a finger at him. Chad just shook his head and ran his hand over his face. Suddenly, she stood up straight and her eyes narrowed. "What do you mean 'was' one of our employees?" she hissed. "Did that little bitch go to work for one of our competitors?"

"Ginger is dead," intervened Frank. He had seen enough of the family feud. He had his job to do too. Nina whirled around and gave him a suspicious look.

"How?" she asked. "When? She has appointments booked!"

Nina snapped.

"Nina, for heaven's sake, the woman is dead!" Chad said, color mounting in his cheeks.

"Well, then somebody better go find someone else to fill her appointments! I can see you are in mourning, so as usual, I'll take care of it!" Nina glared at Chad and turned to walk out the door.

"Just a minute," said Frank, "I have a few questions for you, too," he said, holding her eyes. It was clear she didn't like being challenged. She rolled her eyes and gave him a disgusted sneer.

"Well, Mr. Riley…" she started.

"It's Detective Riley," he threw right back at her.

"Well, Detective," she said, with a tone meant to humiliate, "unless you are going to pay our bills, your questions will have to wait." She threw her chin up and turned to go again, shaking her head.

"You can answer my questions here or down at the station, Mrs. Roberts," he said firmly, "but you will answer them now." He could swear he saw a smile tug at the corner of Chad's mouth as he quickly covered it with a hand.

"How dare you!" she retorted, her face growing red with rage. Her fists were clenched at her sides.

"Sit, or turn around and put your hands behind your back," he replied calmly, but his eyes told her he wasn't kidding. He almost wished she would give him some more trouble so he could haul her away and give Chad a short reprieve. He did not pull a chair out for her, instead, he stood, glaring right back at her. He reached behind his back and brought out his hand cuffs, which he held, dangling from one hand. The action was not lost on her, and she was livid. But she stomped over and threw herself into a chair, crossing her arms across her ample chest.

"Well, what?" she hissed. "I have a business to run!"

Frank took his time replacing the cuffs, pulling out a pad, and sitting down across from her. He looked at Chad, who was still standing in the middle of the small room.

"Thank you, Mr. Roberts, I appreciate your help. I'll be back in touch if I need anything else," he said. Chad hooked a thumb towards the open door, with a question on his face. Frank nodded that he could go, and did not miss the smile on Chad's face as he walked back to the front office.

"Now, Mrs. Roberts, what was your relationship with Ginger Snapper?"

"My relationship?" she repeated. "She was an employee, nothing more!" she spat. He was amused at her indignation. Long aware of the power of a stare combined with silence, Frank simply waited, drilling his eyes into hers. She began to flush a bright red, as she tried to stare him down. When that did not work, she uncrossed her arms and began to drum on the table with finger nails that matched her blood red lips. Frank smiled as she blinked and looked away first. "I'm very busy, Detective," she repeated, with irritation.

"Were you aware that Miss Snapper was allergic to chlorine?" he asked.

"Of course," she snarled, "everyone knew that!"

"Were you also aware that she had asthma and used an inhaler?" He continued to stare at her, sensing something he did not like. Was it just her innate nastiness, or was something else bothering him?

"Yes," she said, sighing with exaggeration. "Really, Detective, this is a waste of my time."

"Where were you last night," he asked blandly. She sat back in shock, her mouth hanging open.

"I was home, taking a nice soak in my jacuzzi, if that is any of your business!" she snapped.

"Can anyone verify that?" Frank asked calmly.

"What are you suggesting, "she flared.

"Just answer the question," he repeated.

"I don't think I like your tone!" she hissed.

Frank leaned towards her until he was inches from her face. To her credit, she did not back away, but he thought he detected a shimmer of moisture on her upper lip. He held the posture for several seconds without speaking.

"I don't care if you don't like my tone, "he whispered, after he was sure he had her full attention. He stood abruptly, and looking down at her, smiled without warmth. "Don't leave town," he spoke quietly.

He could hear her sputtering as he walked out of the room. He grinned to himself. He had no reason to tell her to stay in town, other than he just didn't like her. But he had always wanted to say that, so why not now?

Chapter 8

The drive back to the station was pleasant, reminding him of why he lived in Tahoe. The brilliant blue sky that spread over a deeper blue lake was on his left as he took a little longer to get back to his desk. Turning down Johnson Avenue, he left the picturesque view behind, but still breathed deeply of the fresh, clean air. Living in paradise had its perks!

Back inside the concrete station, he walked back to his desk after refilling his coffee mug. He liked his coffee hot, and years ago he started using his travel mug all day, since it kept the black brew hot longer than an open mug. He sipped in appreciation; the coffee was not yet old enough to taste burned or thick.

He set his travel mug down and reviewed his notes. After a few minutes, he got up and went across the hall to the evidence locker. He felt restless, but could not identify the reason.

"Hey Joe," he greeted the young man behind the desk. "I need to take a look at the evidence brought in on the Snapper death last night." They had not officially declared it a murder, so it was still viewed as a suspicious death.

"Sure Frank," the uniformed officer said, pushing the sign in book towards him. Frank signed, then stepped through the doors as they clicked open behind Joe. It only took a few minutes before he found the box with the case evidence he needed. After opening the box and removing the bag with the inhaler, he returned to the front, where he checked it out of evidence.

His next stop was to drop it off and have them test it for fingerprints. Frank took out his cell phone, captured a picture of the pharmacy information from the sticker on the inhaler, and stepped back to his desk. He dialed the pharmacy number and was put on hold by a machine. Impatient, he tried punching several buttons, including zero, hoping someone would pick up, but was disconnected instead.

"Well, that's just grand," he snorted as he stood up and put on his jacket. Fifteen minutes later, he was standing at the counter at the pharmacy.

"Hi, can I help you?" smiled a woman who didn't look old enough to be out of high school.

"Hi, uh, Jenny," he said, glancing at her name tag and putting on his most winning smile. "I'm Detective Riley, and I wonder if I could ask you a few questions." He pulled out his ID and flipped it open for her to see. Mistake.

"I haven't done anything wrong," she replied, her face a cloud of anxiety. "I didn't know they had weed in the car," she protested. Her eyes were moist as she turned to the counter behind her and glanced at the pharmacist, who was looking in their direction now. "Please!" she whispered, "I need this job to help my Mom raise my younger brothers."

"I'm not here about any of that," said Frank, feeling sorry for the young woman. "Take a deep breath," he urged. Jenny's eyes were big as she inhaled several breaths through her nose and exhaled through pursed, quivering lips. He smiled over her shoulder at the pharmacist, who nodded and smiled back. Frank looked at the young girl, who was clearly upset. He motioned the pharmacist over. "It's alright; I got this," he winked at the young woman, who looked uncertain at the turn of events.

"I'm afraid I put Jenny under more stress than I should have," he apologized to the pharmacist. He looked at Jenny. "I was asking for information about a patient, and Jenny was telling me she was not sure she should be the one to answer." The pharmacist looked between the two, and nodded. "I think I put her in a bad position. I'm sorry," he said, smiling at the girl, who offered a weak smile in return. "Too little sleep," he grinned.

"Sounds like you did the right thing, Jenny," said the pharmacist, smiling at the young woman. "I'm Pete Ford, the head pharmacist here. How can I help you?"

Frank glanced at Jenny, who still stood at the counter. He turned his attention back to Pete. He pulled up the picture of the pharmacy sticker on his phone and turned it towards the man.

"I am investigating the death of this young woman, Ginger Snapper," he said, noting the look of surprise that crossed the face of the pharmacist. "Can you pull up her records, please?" Pete moved to the computer on the counter and typed in some information.

"I'm going to bag those prescriptions," Jenny murmured, gesturing toward the few bottles sitting on the counter by the pharmacist station. Pete nodded, without even looking in her direction. She melted quietly into the background, but just before she turned to step up to the pharmacist station to pick up the prescriptions, she caught Frank's eye and mouthed the words "thank you." He smiled. Maybe he made one less young person afraid of the police today.

"Are you looking for anything in particular," asked Pete, meeting his eyes.

"Yes," replied Frank, "I am looking for the history of refills on her asthma inhaler."

"It looks like she refilled this inhaler three days ago."

"Did she ever fill an order for more than one inhaler at a time?" he asked.

"Yes," answered Pete, "her doctor allowed her to have up to three at a time. She was really concerned about being caught without one," continued the pharmacist.

"Was her asthma really severe?" asked Frank, looking for more explanations.

"Her asthma was not as bad as some, but she told me once that her job had her dress in costumes that did not always allow her to have her inhaler on her person. She liked to keep one in her car, one at home, and one at work so she always had one handy in case something triggered a problem." He was silent as he peered at the screen. "She refilled this one three days ago under a special request." He tapped a few more keys. "She said the one she kept in her locker at work had somehow disappeared." He looked at Frank expectantly.

"Disappeared?" repeated Frank.

"Yes," said Pete, she was worried about where she might have left it and concerned about not having one at work."

"Thank you. You've been very helpful," said Frank. He turned and walked towards the door, digesting this new information. What happened to her inhaler? Was the one in the bathroom the one taken from her locker? The next question was, who would have had access?

Chapter 9

Frank headed back to Ginger's apartment. He wanted to take another look for himself. He drove up to the building this time, and noticed Jim out front, sweeping the walkways in front of the apartments.

"Hi Jim," he said as he got out of the car. Jim stopped sweeping and stood, waiting for the detective to get closer. There was a sadness still lingering in the man's eyes.

"Hello, Detective," he said. "What can I do for you?

"I want to look around Ginger's apartment again," answered Frank, "and I would appreciate it if you could let me in."

"Sure," said Jim, not moving anything but his eyes as they scanned over to her front door.

"I'd also like to take a look at that water heater, "he said. "is it around the back?"

Jim looked back at Frank, nodded, then started walking slowly over to the apartment. He hesitated in front of the door, then glanced at Frank. "Let's look at that water heater first," he said.

The two men walked around to the back of the building to a small closet type structure attached to the side of the building. He pulled the latch on the door back and opened the cabinet, revealing two water heaters, side by side, elevated slightly on a small concrete platform. Each one had a number on it, written in permanent marker.

"That's the one for Ginger's apartment," Jim said, pointing to the one closest to her apartment. Frank stepped forward to have a closer look.

"There is no lock on the cabinet door?" he asked.

"No," said Jim, "never thought there was a need." He glanced at Frank, then back at the water heaters. "I always wanted someone to be able to get to them if I was away for some reason and they needed to be fixed or adjusted."

Frank stepped up on the rim of the concrete stoop that held the water heaters. He looked around the top and sides. "Could the water line be tampered with to add in chlorine?" he asked. Jim thought for a few minutes, chewing on his lip.

"I don't see how," he said. "They would have to go under the building in the crawl space and tap into the water line. That would take a lot of time and I can't imagine I wouldn't see them. I am around the premises all day."

"Did you leave the property at any time in the past few days?" asked Frank.

"No," said Jim, rubbing his chin in thought, for several seconds. "No," he said emphatically, "and besides, the Clancy's don't get out much anymore, so they sit by their window and look outside a lot." Jim knitted his eyebrows together as if he were concentrating. "It would also have to be someone that really knew what they were doing. Not just anyone can do plumbing." Frank stepped down from the stoop and stood for a few minutes.

"Okay," he said, "let's go look inside."

Jim led the way around to the front of the building,   digging at the key ring on his belt as he walked. He sighed as he slipped the key in the door and opened it, looked at Frank, hesitated, then stepped through the door ahead of the detective.

It took Frank's eyes a few minutes to adjust to the darkened interior. He looked at the blinds, and without a word, Jim stepped over and opened them. Frank methodically took in every piece of furniture, every knick knack.

"Shoot! Not again! I told Ginger I needed…" Jim's voice broke off and he looked at Frank, then walked over to the back door of the apartment. The door was ever so slightly out of place. "I didn't notice when we walked around back, but I guess I forgot to bolt the door after they took her away last night." He passed his hand over his face.

"Bolt the door?" asked Frank, looking at the area. It was hardly noticeable; the door was still in the frame, but not tight.

"Yeah. See here?" said Jim, pointing to the door jamb. Frank looked over his shoulder. "The wood is rotten in the door jamb. Too many years of exposure to weather, being on the end of the building." He shook his head. "I told Ginger I wanted to replace the door frame, but she wouldn't have it."

"Why not?" asked Frank, still not sure that it mattered.

"She loved this door with the little window that opened in the summer. I can't get those anymore; it is more narrow than the doors they make today. I would have had to widen and replace the door frame and get a bigger door, but I couldn't get one with a window." He sighed. "Darn thing was always coming open. Unless Ginger remembered to flip the dead bolt, the slightest breeze would push the door open."

Frank's attention sharpened. He walked over to the door and

examined the frame. The latch strike was worn thin, and the wood inside the casing was rotten and crumbling. He pushed the door shut, then pulled the knob lightly towards him without turning. The door came open at the gentle pressure.

He stood for a minute staring at the latch, then turned and walked through the apartment to the bathroom. He put on plastic gloves he removed from his pocket, flipped on the light, and stepped inside the bathroom.

"Sorry," said Jim, gesturing toward the door that still hung from one hinge. "I just haven't wanted to come back in here."

"Don't worry about it," said Frank, smiling back at the stricken man standing on the other side of the door. He turned his attention back to the task at hand and moved the door so he could look at the sliding bolt lock on the back of the door.   "I think I broke that when I kicked the door open," said Jim quietly.

The slider hung by one screw in the back of the door. Frank noted it was bent, and holding it against the door with one hand, he tried to slide the lock. It stuck, and he had to jiggle it hard to make it move. *Could that have prevented Ginger from getting out?* He took a small pen light out of his pocket and knelt down to look in the receptacle. It looked normal, except…there was a shine to the wood at the back of the indentation.

"Has the inside of this latch strike been varnished?" asked Frank. Jim gave him a blank look.

"No," he replied slowly, shaking his head. "I have only owned this place for the past six years, but I have never heard of varnishing or even priming the inside of a latch strike."

"Huh." Frank took out his pocket knife and a small, plastic bag, and scratched a bit of wood from the inside of the latch strike. He deposited the result of his effort into the small bag, then turned his flashlight to the end of the sliding bar on the latch. It was shiny too. The rest of the bar looked on the verge of rusting. He jiggled the bar again to get it to slide. He held the bag open beneath the latch bar and used his knife to scrape a little of the shiny coating into the bag.

"Did you find something?" asked Jim.

"I don't know yet," replied Frank absently as he stood and gazed at the closed window. He could see tiny specks of what was likely blood on the frame of the window, and a few streaks of copper coloring along the wall under the window. Carefully, he stepped into the tub and peered closely at the window frame. He lifted his pen light and directed the light around the frame. There was a shiny substance barely discernible around the rim of the frame. He slipped his light back in his pocket and used both hands to tug at the window. It did not move.

"Ginger never said anything about that window sticking," said Jim, behind Frank. "That is a dual pane window and frame I put in about a year ago. She was real glad for the extra warmth in the winter, but she never said it got stuck."

"Maybe it didn't," offered Frank, taking out another little bag and his pocket knife again. He scraped a small amount of the shiny substance off the frame of the window, in several places, then placed that bag in his other pocket.

The detective stood perfectly still, slowly moving his eyes over the area. They stopped on the shower head.

"Do you have a paper towel or a piece of newspaper?" he asked Jim.

"Sure, there is a towel rack in the kitchen. I'll get one." He was back shortly with two paper towels, still connected to each other. He handed them to Frank, who carefully moved back a step so he wasn't directly under the head. He bent over and placed the paper towels in the tub, underneath the shower. He reached up and slowly loosened the shower head. A fine, barely detectable amount of white powder drifted downward. Frank removed the shower head completely and looked inside the metal plumbing fixture.

"Do you have a lot of lime deposit build up here?" he asked Jim.

"Not really," he shrugged. "Once a year I use a tablet from H2O to dissolve the little bit we get here, but that is for the toilets. I use a spray on the faucets, but never on the shower heads."

"I'm going to take all of this to the lab, just to be sure," Frank said, wrapping the shower head in the paper towels and carefully placing the whole bundle in a bigger plastic bag he took out of his inside coat pocket. He peered up inside the shower pipe and pulled his flashlight out of his pocket again. Exchanging the flashlight for his pocket knife, Frank held the plastic bag under the pipe with one hand and scraped the small knife inside the pipe. More fine white powder fell into the bag.

He had already stepped out of the tub enclosure when he noticed one of the handles on the faucets lying in the bottom of the tub. He bent to examine it and lifted it to look inside the receptacle. It looked like the inside was stripped. He reached over and touched the other knob and it came off in his hand.

"What the heck?" said Jim. "Ginger never said anything about the knobs coming off either," he stammered. "I run a good place here, Detective, I keep things up!" He was obviously flustered.

"Do you mind if I take these with me?" asked Frank, purely out of courtesy. He was already wrapping them in a clean handkerchief he took out of his breast pocket.

"I…but…no, of course not, if you think it will help," Jim said, resignation coming through in his voice. He looked at Frank with fear in his eyes. "Detective, what is going on here?" he asked.

"I'm not sure yet, Jim. But don't let anyone in here except me." Jim nodded and Frank moved out of the bathroom, stripping his plastic gloves off. He led the way to the front door and watched as Jim secured the lock. "Thanks for your help," he said, starting back to his car.

"Detective Riley?"

"Yes," he said, turning back to face Jim.

"Should I be worried for the safety of my tenants?" asked Jim.

Frank hesitated, examining the ashen face and frightened eyes. He softened as Jim glanced towards the Clancey apartment. "I would be extra cautious and tell everyone to keep their doors and windows locked when they are out and at night," he said. He turned away again.

"Detective Riley?" asked Jim again.

"Yes?" he responded patiently, turning around one more time.

"You don't think this was an accident, do you." It was a statement, not a question.

"No, Jim, I'm afraid I don't," Frank said quietly. He met Jim's eyes honestly.

"Who would want to hurt Ginger?" Jim asked, his eyes brimming with tears.

"That's what I'm going to find out, Jim," Frank said. "I'm going to do everything I can to get that answer for you." This time when he started for his car, there were no more questions. He set the knobs carefully on the passenger seat and got in the car. He started the engine and pulled out, glancing once more back at the apartment building. Jim was still standing in the lot, hands on his hips, staring at him as he drove away.

Chapter 10

Frank's stomach rumbled and the thought of a turkey avocado bacon sandwich from the Tahoe Keys Deli was too tempting to resist. He pulled off the highway into the small parking area in front of the popular stop. He was not surprised to see it was busy, with three customers ahead of him in the tiny space, but he knew it would be worth the wait.   He took his sandwich and a soft drink back to the station and sat at his desk, eating his lunch while his mind mulled over the details of the morning. He wadded up the waxed paper and threw it in the wastebasket as he stood. He stuffed the knobs in one pocket, still wrapped in the cloth, and checked to make sure he had all the baggies with the scrapings. Frank drained the can of soda and then walked towards the door, dropping the can in the recycling bin on his way outside.

The day was usually bright and the sun felt good on his back. He watched two squirrels chase each other around and up a tree in the middle of the lawn. He decided he spent too much time inside and needed to take a day and go for a hike – maybe up to Eagle Falls or around Fallen Leaf. It was so peaceful there. Both areas had views of pristine lakes and offered solitude, although Fallen Leaf required a greater sense of adventure to navigate the dusty, pitted, narrow road to hiking areas. He would make one of those hikes a priority before the snow flew and blocked the access.

Frank blinked as he came out of the sunlight and into the softer light of the lab, where Bruce was sitting at his computer. Bruce looked up and smiled as Frank came through the door.

"How's it going?" asked Bruce, noting the bulge in Frank's pocket.

"I've got a few things I'd like you to test for me," Frank answered, pulling the baggies and the knobs out of his pockets and laying them on the desk. Bruce reached for a clip board hanging on a hook beside his desk.

"Talk to me, "he said, writing the date and Frank's name on the top of the page. "Are these connected to an existing case?"

"Yeah," answered the detective, "I took the scrapings in bag A from around the window in the apartment of Ginger Snapper." Bruce looked at Frank. "The window was stuck, and I want to know if this substance had anything to do with the window not opening." Bruce nodded as he took notes.

"You think it could be a sealant of some kind?" asked Bruce, studying Frank's face.

"Yeah. I couldn't open the window either." Frank handed the baggie to Bruce, who put it in its own sleeve. "These," he said, indicating the baggie with a B written on the outside, "came from the bolt of a slide lock and the interior of the receptacle." Bruce took the second packet and put it in a separate sleeve. He pointed to the knobs lying on the cloth and gave Frank a questioning look. "Those came off in my hand," he continued. "Looks like they might be stripped inside so they wouldn't turn off the water, so see if you can find any substance inside to indicate they might have been altered." Bruce leaned over and opened a drawer, from which he pulled another plastic bag. He used the bag itself to surround the knobs and then closed the bag around them.

"Looks like you have something else for me," said the lab tech, gesturing toward the other bag in Frank's hand.

"Check the substance inside the shower head, which is wrapped in the paper towels. There is a little more residue in the bag from scraping the inside of the pipe."

"You want to know if the white powder is all the same substance," said Bruce.

"And what that substance is," finished Frank. "Be careful," added Frank, "it could be toxic."

"Careful is my middle name," said Bruce, grinning. His face became somber again. "So," Bruce said slowly, "it sounds like you don't think this was an accident."

"No," Frank answered, his mouth setting in a grim line."I think we have a homicide on our hands."

"I'll push this to the front of the line, then." He studied Frank's solemn face, then added: "I'll let you know as soon as I have something." Frank turned and headed out the door and back to his office.

"Thanks, Bruce, I appreciate it."

Chapter 11

Frank sat at his desk, staring at the computer screen. He felt dry, like he couldn't get past this point. A young woman was dead. She seemed to be well liked, except maybe by Nina, who didn't seem to like anyone. There was too much evidence to look at anything but murder, but why? What was the motive?

He had done a quick search on the building owner, just to be sure. Jim was clean, no criminal record, not even a speeding ticket. The Clancy's were not physically well, and they liked Ginger, but he checked them out none the less.

"Well, look at that!" he exclaimed. "Bless you for your service, Sir," he said to himself. Carey Clancy had been awarded the Purple Heart for his military service in Korea.

He began to check on Ginger's background. Maybe there was something there that would open a door. He read with sadness about the young woman's past. Orphaned when her parents were both killed in a plane crash, then raised by her grandmother. That coincided with what Chad had said about the young woman.

He continued reading; her grandmother was a foster parent and had raised Ginger with other hapless children she had taken in. *The woman was capable of giving a lot of love to the forlorn.* The Grandmother passed away a few years back. Frank shook his head. It amazed him to see what some people had to endure to survive.

He typed in Nina Roberts next. Hmm. "Now that is interesting! Nina Roberts, why do you have a sealed record? What did you do?" He was attempting to navigate through the complicated system, looking for at least a name that he could call for information, when the voice of his Captain jerked him away from his thoughts.

"Frank!" yelled his Captain across the room. Frank looked up to see him motion the detective to his office. The Captain did not wait for Frank before he went back inside his office. Frank followed his boss into the office, where the man was already back behind his desk. He was reading a sheet of paper.

"What's up, Captain? "asked Frank, stepping into the crowded office.

"This just came across my desk," he said, handing Frank a sheet of paper. "Another employee at 'We Do It Your Way' just had a bad incident. Could be it relates to your murder case." He fixed Frank with a grim smile. So the Captain thought it was murder too, Frank noted.

"I'll get on it," said Frank, turning back to his desk. He closed his screen down and grabbed his coat. He was in his car and headed to the address on the paper in less than ten minutes.

Chapter 12

The ambulance was just closing the doors as he got to the building supply company. Frank heard the siren start cranking and watched as the ambulance pulled out on the highway. He scanned the scene and singled out the uniformed officer standing to the side, note pad out, talking to two men who looked shaken.

"Detective Riley," he said flashing his shield and nodding at the officer. The officer shot him a glance and looked at the two men, then back to Frank.

"Rayburn, Sir," stated the officer, gesturing in the direction of the men. It was an unspoken question.

"Continue," said Frank, giving permission to the younger officer to proceed.

"This is Jerry," Rayburn said, waving a hand towards a tall, thin young man, "and this is Clyde," he said, indicating the shorter of the two construction workers. The men nodded at Frank.

What else can you tell me?" the officer asked, studying Jerry's face.

"We hired a woman to come and sing to the boss for his birthday," he said.

"Can you tell me her name?" asked Frank.

"Just her first name," answered Clyde. "She just said her name was Stephanie." *The young Nurse Ratchet from "We Do It Your Way."* He looked at the men and waited expectantly.

"Anyway," continued Jerry, "the boss has a huge crush on Taylor Swift, so we picked a girl that looked like her and she was all dressed in this gorgeous red lace dress with heels that lit up red when she walked." He took his hard hat off and smoothed back his dark hair. He was tall and wiry, and wore a tool belt slung low over his hips. "She looked so beautiful; we knew the boss would be happy!" He rubbed a hand over his tanned face and looked up, moving his eyes from Frank to the other officer. "She was all ready to jump out and surprise the boss. "

"She was going to sing his favorite song, and get him to two step a little dance for his birthday," added Clyde, who was a few inches shorter in stature, but definitely well muscled. He pinched the bridge of his nose and shook his head. "We thought it would be so cool," he continued, his brows knitted together over eyes that showed concern.

"We were all ready, but at the last minute, she grabbed her stomach and said she didn't feel good," said Jerry. He chewed on his lip, moving his eyes from Frank to the other officer. "It was awful."

"What happened next?" asked Frank.

"Her lips turned blue," said Jerry.

"And then she started vomiting blood," added Clyde. "I've never seen anything like it." The two workers exchanged a look of misery, then both turned their gaze to Frank.

"Did you see her take anything to drink, or eat anything before she got sick?" he asked.

"Just some water," replied Jerry.

"Where did she get the water?" asked Frank.

"She had a water bottle with her," said Clyde. "She set it down right over there," he pointed, "On that stack of lumber. The blue metal bottle." Frank followed the man's finger and then locked eyes with the other officer, who nodded silent understanding and walked over to retrieve the water bottle.

"I called an ambulance right away," said Jerry nervously. "I didn't know what else to do."

"I had a clean handkerchief I gave her," said Clyde. He shook his head. "She pretty much soaked that with blood in a few minutes time." He turned worried eyes at Frank. "She was screaming from the pain." He looked down at his boots and the two construction workers were quiet while Frank and Officer Rayburn waited.

"Is she gonna make it?" Jerry finally asked.

"I can't answer that," Frank said honestly. "We have your contact information though, right?"

"Yes," replied Clyde, looking first at Jerry, then at Officer Rayburn.

"I'll give you a call as soon as I know her condition," Frank offered. It wasn't protocol, but he understood. The witnesses often were left to wonder the outcome. These men were obviously affected by what they had seen.

"Can we go?" asked Jerry.

"Yes," answered Frank. He watched the two young men walk away, heads down. It was a nasty thing for them to see.

"Do you want me to take this to the lab, Sir?" asked Rayburn, holding up a plastic bag with a metallic blue water bottle inside.

"No," said Frank thoughtfully, "thanks, but I need to check with

Bruce or the ME anyway, so I'll take it over." Rayburn nodded, then started to walk back to his unit. "Hey, Rayburn?" said Frank.

"Yes, Sir?" answered the young officer.

"There is something you can do for me." The officer nodded expectantly. Frank took out his notebook and wrote an address and a name on a sheet of paper, then ripped it out and handed it to the other man. "Pick this guy up and bring him down for questioning. If he isn't at that address, they should be able to tell you where to find him."

"Copy that," said Rayburn, continuing back to his unit.

Frank blew out a long breath, then walked back to his own vehicle. If this kept up, the Medical Examiner's office was going to be working a lot of overtime.

Chapter 13

Ken sat at the table in the interrogation room. The young fire fighter imitator was fidgeting; tapping his foot and clenching and unclenching his hands. Frank let him sit as he watched through the mirror, noting he rubbed his hands over his face and through his hair often. He was clearly uncomfortable.

Frank looked at his phone, then let Ken sit for another five minutes before opening the door. Without a word, he walked into the room, carrying a brown paper lunch bag. He set the bag on the table and sat down across from Ken. The man sat up and looked expectantly at Frank. The Detective sat down and just stared at him, without saying a word.

"What?'' he asked. Frank didn't even blink. "Why am I here?" Ken was flustered. His eyes darted around the bare room and then came back to rest on Frank's face. He scrunched up his eyes and leaned forward. "Hey! I know you!" He pointed at Frank. "You were at the office this morning!" Frank nodded, but said nothing. "You can't hold me here!" he declared.

Frank reached in the paper bag and brought out a clear evidence bag, which he put, with a metallic blue water bottle, on the table. His eyes were locked on Ken's.

"That's Stephanie's water bottle!" He looked from the bottle to Frank. "What are you doing with her water bottle?"

"How do you know it's Stephanie's?"

"See that?" Ken pointed to a small scratch on one side of the bottle. "She was excited when she bought it. It is a very expensive brand, but that little scratch made it cost less than half price."

"When is the last time you saw this?' asked Frank.

"At the office, when I filled it up for Stephanie!" he said belligerently. "Why did you take it from her?" He grabbed for the bottle, but Frank was faster. "Gimmee that, it's not yours!" His face was red now.

"What did you put in the water bottle, Ken?" asked Frank quietly.

"What? Water!" His face twisted in puzzlement for a few seconds as he stared at the detective. Then he shook his head. "You were there! Give it to me and I'll take it back to Stephanie!"

"What kind of poison was it, Ken?" Frank did not have the lab tests back yet, but it was worth a try.

"Poison?" Ken's face contorted as he stared at Frank. "What are you talking about?"

"Stephanie," said Frank, "what kind of poison did you put in her water bottle?"

"That's crazy talk," the young man said impatiently, "why would I…" He stopped, and his face turned pale. "What are you saying? Did something happen to Stephanie?" he gasped.

"What did you do to her?" asked Frank.

"Nothing! Where is she? Is she alright?" Ken stood up and started for the door, but Frank was suddenly standing in front of him.

"She's at Barton Hospital," said Frank, watching Ken for his reaction.

"No! No, that can't be!" He staggered back and crumpled into the chair. He stared at the floor for a few minutes, then jumped to his feet again. "You have to let me go to her!" he pleaded.

"Your fingerprints were on the water bottle, Ken."

"Of course they were! You saw me fill it for her!" Tears started down his cheeks. "Please," he begged, "let me go to her. I wouldn't hurt her." He wiped the tears off his face with one hand, then looked imploringly at Frank. "Please," he whispered. " I love her!"

Frank stepped aside and opened the door. "Let's go," he said.

"You'll let me see her?"Ken studied the detective's face. "Please," he begged.

"I'll give you a ride," said Frank. He was inclined to believe the young man, but he still wanted to see Stephanie's reaction when she saw Ken.

Chapter 14

Ken sat silently, staring straight ahead, as Frank drove to the hospital. Frank had no real reason to cuff him, so he rode in the front passenger seat of the unmarked car. At the entrance to the hospital, Frank waited while the young man got quickly out of the car. Ken was definitely pale, but why remained to be seen.

The sliding doors opened and they walked through the lobby to the elevator, where they rode to the second floor in silence. The doors slid open and they stepped out into an open area with a circular desk in the middle. They were met by a tall, muscular male nurse in scrubs. His brown hair was cut short and his eyes were clear; everything about him said no nonsense allowed.

"May I help you," he asked evenly, studying them both carefully. His legs were spread wide and his hands were at his sides. At that moment, he looked more like a linebacker bracing the offense than a nurse, and it was clear no one was going to walk by him without a challenge.

"Detective Frank Riley," he explained, showing his badge to the young nurse. He looked at the nurse's name badge. "Brian, can you tell me where we can find Stephanie…" Frank stopped, realizing he did not know her last name.

"Stephanie Devers," interjected Ken.

Brian visibly relaxed. "The officer told me there would be a guard sent up here to stand by her room shortly," he said. "It doesn't take a rocket scientist to figure out something must have happened to her that gave the officers reason to post a guard. I didn't know who you were, but…" he stopped, and gave Frank a sheepish grin. "I played defense in college football, so I was going to give it my best shot to protect her."

"You did the right thing," said Frank, smiling at the young man. "She could be in danger." Brian nodded and turned to walk down the hall behind him.

"She's down here in the last room on the right," he said. "It's more secure," he added, stopping in front of the door and motioning towards the bed. "We have her in here alone, too." The nurse stepped in ahead of them and walked to the far side of the bed, where he began to check monitors and intravenous lines.

Stephanie lay in the bed, looking very pale and small underneath the thin covers. Ken made a choking sound, then stepped forward and slowly, gently took her hand in his. He bent to kiss her hand, keeping his eyes on her face.

"Oh, Stephanie," he breathed quietly, "who did this to you?" Stephanie started to stir as he stroked her hand. Her eyes fluttered, then closed again. "Stephanie?" said Ken. Her eyes opened again and Frank saw her start to focus on Ken's face. Then her eyes got big.

"Get away from me!" she hissed. "It was you, wasn't it?" she cried hoarsely.

"No, Stephanie, I didn't…," began Ken. Frank pulled his cuffs off his belt and yanked Ken backwards as nurse Hodge stepped around the bed to put himself between Stephanie and Ken.

"Let's go!" commanded Frank, pushing Ken ahead of him, out of the room.

"No! Stephanie!" cried Ken. "I wouldn't hurt you!"

"Be quiet, you're in a hospital!" growled Frank, pushing him against the wall and jamming his wrists into the handcuffs. Pulling him through the door, he half dragged him down the hall to the elevator. Frank hit the down button and they waited in silence until the door opened and Frank led Ken inside.

"But, I didn't…!" protested Ken.

"You have the right to remain silent," began Frank, and I suggest right now you do just that!" He half shoved, half pulled a limp Ken through the lobby to his car. He finished the Miranda rights before he opened the door and guided Ken into the back seat. He called for another unit to transport and stood outside the car, rubbing his hand over his eyes. Something was bothering him, but he couldn't quite put his finger on it.

A patrol unit pulled up and Frank opened the door while they transferred Ken to the car.

"I didn't do anything!" said Ken. Frank looked at the officers.

"Hold him until I get back in to question him. It might be tomorrow." The officer nodded and took Ken over to his cruiser. Frank stood, watching them put him in the car. Bed sounded good. He needed time to process, and sometimes, he did his best work while he slept.

Chapter 15

At a quarter to seven the next morning, Frank was waiting when Sierra walked through the door.

"Detective," she said, a little surprise showing in her voice. "And coffee," she said, her eyes moving to the two cups of coffee Frank held, then back up to his face.

"Good coffee," said Frank, smiling, as he extended a cup of Alpina coffee towards her.

"Thank you," she smiled back, "and I am sure there is a price tag attached to this display of early morning cordiality." She lifted an eyebrow in his direction.

"Well, actually," Frank grinned sheepishly, "I was hoping to run some ideas by you." He held up a bag. "Muffins."

"Blueberry?"

"And orange cranberry."

"Let's talk," she said, leading the way down the hall to the break room. "Unless…," she hesitated, an impish smirk on her face, "you prefer a colder place?"

"No, this will be fine," answered Frank, as he spread napkins on the small table. He tore the side of the bag open to reveal four plump muffins. An aroma of spices permeated the room. Sierra reached out and took a blueberry muffin. She closed her eyes and sniffed as she held the baked treat close to her nose, then smiled, and broke a piece off, beginning to nibble.

"So, fire away," she said, settling back in the chair. She answered his questions honestly and asked a few of her own for the better part of two hours. Frank felt like he was forging a good working relationship with the new ME, when suddenly he remembered the night he had seen her wipe away a tear on the way to her car.

"Sierra," he began, "the day we met, I was in the parking lot getting ready to go home late at night. I saw you come out of the building and…it looked like you were crying." In an instant, her face froze for and her smile was gone. "I mean, I don't want to pry, but is there any way I can help?" He was too good a detective not to know he had made a crucial error in judgment; he had trespassed into forbidden personal territory. The coffee turned to acid in his stomach as he watched the invisible barrier go back up.

"Are you stalking me?" Her eyes flashed with anger as she slammed the empty paper cup onto the table. He turned his palms out and shook his head back and forth, at a total loss for words. "I have to get back to work," she said, standing abruptly and gathering the cups, then tossing them in the trash on her way out the door. Frank looked at the lone remaining muffin and blew out a breath.

"You're an idiot, Riley!" he muttered as he stood, leaving the muffin on the table. He kicked himself all the way over to the office of "We Do It Your Way."

Chapter 16

Frank opened the door to the business and was met with silence. He knew Stephanie would not be at her desk, but he thought someone would be in the office, especially since the door was unlocked. He walked into the main room and called hello, but there was no answer. He stood still, listening, but heard nothing. *Odd. Someone should be here – the door is unlocked.*

Frustrated, he began to lift items on Stephanie's desk, and even edged both drawers out carefully. Nothing unusual. He continued down the hall and was in the locker room, opening any unlocked lockers quietly, when he heard a door in the back of the building slam a minute before Nina stomped into the room. Stopping short, she glared at him.

"Oh! I thought you were Ken!" Her surprise seemed genuine, but Frank simply stood, holding her gaze. "What do you think you are doing?" she demanded, recovering from her momentary shock.

"Good, you can open this for me, I assume," Frank countered, pointing to the locker that had Ken's name on the front.

Nina's mouth fell open as she gawked at him. Color rose in her cheeks as she regained her composure. "How dare you!" she fumed. Her eyes narrowed to slits. "Do you have a warrant?" she hissed.

"No," Frank said softly, stepping closer to her. She stepped back and he smiled to himself. Old technique, but worked to force people off guard. "I can get one, but you won't like it."

"Well, you better go get it and don't come back until you do!" she snarled. Frank did not move.

"One of your employees is dead, another is in the hospital," he said, watching her face carefully for a reaction. "And one is in jail." He dropped the last bit of information as he scrutinized her face. "Is there anything you want to tell me, Mrs. Roberts?" Frank stared at her, keeping his expression impassive.

"What do you mean by that?" She shifted from one foot to the other, then seemed to recover. The phone rang down the hall, and she stared in that direction with fury flashing in her eyes. The ringing stopped. "Stephanie didn't show up for work today, so I have to do everything myself again!" Turning back to Frank, she actually growled at him! "I can't find Chad and Ken isn't answering his phone!" The phone rang in the front office again and Nina turned with obvious irritation and stormed back down the hall. Frank followed.

"We do it Your Way," she cooed into the phone. Listening while she glared at Frank, she bent and picked up a pen, then wrote something on a piece of paper. "I'll get back to you by this afternoon," she continued, her voice thick with sweetness. She dropped the phone back into the cradle and turned to face him. Her mouth twisted into a snarl and placing her hands on her hips, she opened her mouth. But no words came out. Realization faded across her face and she stood, her mouth gaping open, as she finally processed what he had said in the locker room.

"Wait. What do you mean I have an employee in the hospital and one in jail?" For the first time since Frank had met the woman, she was passive. "I don't understand," she said, shaking her head from side to side. He let the silence hang in the air for a few minutes as he studied her.

"Stephanie is in the hospital," he said simply.

"She can't be! I need her here!" Nina caught herself. "I mean…what happened? Is she alright?" she stared blandly at Frank.

"It appears she was poisoned," he stated. Nina's expression did not change. She's a cold cookie, alright, thought Frank, as he watched her processing behind the mask.

"Poisoned." It was a statement. Nina drew in a breath and held it for several seconds, before exhaling carefully.

"Is Chad in jail?" she asked softly.

"No," answered Frank, hiding his surprise at the question. "We have Ken in custody." Nina sank into the chair beside the desk and stared at the floor. Frank stood silently.

"What is going on?" she asked, more subdued than he had ever seen her.

"Stephanie is in the hospital, with what they believe is arsenic poisoning. We are holding Ken for questioning." The color had drained out of her face, making her heavy makeup look garish. He pulled another chair over closer and sat down, taking out his note pad.

"Now, what can you tell me about the job Stephanie was sent to yesterday afternoon?" he queried. She swiveled the chair to face the desk and opened the planner. Her finger traced the writing on the date, then she turned and pulled out a file from the drawer in the side of the desk.

"Nothing unusual," she said, plopping the file in front of him.

Two guys named Clyde and Jerry booked a birthday song and dance for their boss. That's what we have on them," she said, pushing the file towards him.

Frank skimmed the file and realized there was nothing in it that he didn't already know. He studied Nina, who was still shaking her head back and forth and blinking frequently, as if trying to focus.

"Have you had any issues with rodents?" Frank asked suddenly.

"Of course not!" Nina said, her head snapping up to glare at him. "We keep things clean around here! What the hell does that have to do with anything?" Frank just stared at her. She was either a really good actress or she did not make the connection.

"Ken's locker?" He repeated the earlier request. She sighed, then rose and led the way back to the locker room. She opened her own locker and took out a key ring. She looked at Frank.

"We give them a lock and key, but they don't know we have a master key," she said with apparent satisfaction as she slipped the key in and opened the lock. She opened the door to the locker, looked inside, then stepped back.

Frank pulled on plastic gloves, then stepped in front of the locker and rummaged through the sparse belongings inside. He found deodorant, a razor, a white tee shirt and gym shorts, and a bottle of pills. He pulled the bottle out and read the label. It was a prescription for antibiotics, that Ken had apparently not taken for the fully prescribed time. He started to return it to the locker, then hesitated. He looked at Nina and held up the bottle.

"I'm taking this to the lab, just to be sure," he said, depositing the brown plastic container in an evidence bag. She merely shrugged her shoulders. The phone rang again.

"Is there anything else, Detective?" she asked quietly. For once, she seemed almost beaten. "I really have to find out where Chad and Michelle are and get my business back in order."

"I'll be in touch," he said, pocketing the pills and walking towards the front door. He glanced back at Nina as she picked up the phone and began to punch buttons. She looked haggard. And why did she ask if Chad was in jail?

Chapter 17

For the second time that day Frank walked into the building that housed the ME, carrying food. It was lunch time and he brought Bruce some sliders and sweet potato fries from Sonney's Barbecue, a favorite of the Assistant ME. His own stomach was rumbling as he walked through the doors, and he hoped Bruce hadn't eaten. He usually got more conversation from the ME's office when he brought food, although after this morning, he might have to rethink his approach.

"Frank!"exclaimed Bruce, coming down the hall as the detective approached his desk. "I was just going to give you a call." He stopped and eyed the bag in Frank's hands. The tantalizing aroma wafted into the air surrounding his desk. "Is that what I think it is?" he ventured hopefully.

"Yes, it is!" grinned Frank, I am starving and was hoping we could exchange information over lunch."

"Don't tell Cecelia I didn't eat that peanut butter sandwich she sent today," laughed Bruce. She was up all night with the kids, but still wanted to make me something for lunch. She's old fashioned that way, even though she works too! Come on," he motioned in the direction of the bag. "I'm literally going to start drooling in a minute!"

Frank pulled up a chair to his desk and reached into the bag and withdrew two paper plates. "I asked them to set us up," he grinned, handing Bruce a couple of napkins. He also withdrew two cans of soda and placed one in front of each of them. Next, he tore open the side of the bag to reveal several sliders and a double order of sweet potato fries. "Dig in!"

The two men ate silently for a few minutes, both very hungry and focused on the food. After the second slider, Frank looked at Bruce with a question on his face. Bruce nodded as he swallowed.

"Let's start with the chlorine," he said. There were two tablets jammed inside the shower head."

"So someone had to have access," stated Frank.

"Yes," agreed Bruce, "and I would think it would take a few minutes to unscrew the head and jam the tablets inside."

"Unfortunately," said Frank, "access was probably easy. It was an end unit with a back door that wouldn't always stay closed." He thought for a minute.

"Those chlorine tablets are easy to get at any pool or spa supply store," said Bruce, thinking out loud. Frank nodded.

"Did you get anything out of the other scrapings?"

"Yes," Bruce replied. "Someone wanted to make sure she could not get out in time." Bruce sighed. "Nasty jobs we have. Someone put Gorilla glue around the edge of the window, and in the lock and strike." He looked at a third slider and Frank gestured for him to go ahead. Bruce picked it up and took a bite before meeting Frank's eyes.

"Someone also filed the threads off the screws in the tub handles," Bruce continued. "They used an ordinary glue to set the handles back on, so they would work to turn the water on, but would be too weak to hold the handles on when she tried to turn off the water."

"Obviously, it was someone who knew she was allergic to chlorine," mused Frank, "then made sure she would be trapped in the bathroom long enough to put her in danger." He looked at Bruce. "They also loosened the screws holding the slider lock in place, so when she grabbed at the slider, it came loose and practically fell off the door."

"That is cold blooded, premeditated murder," said Bruce. Both men were silent for several moments. "But, why?" asked Bruce.

"That's what I don't have; a motive," said Frank. He bit his lower lip, deep in thought. "Everyone I talked to seemed to love Ginger," he stated, "except maybe the female owner of the business. But then, she doesn't seem to like anyone. She is a very unhappy and cantankerous person."

"What has happened to her to make her so unhappy?" asked Bruce. "Most people aren't born that way," he speculated, looking at Frank.

"Well, partner," he smiled wanly, "that's what I need to find out. I guess that's why I'm the detective," he grinned. Frank stood and started to pick up the debris from their lunch. "Oh!" he said, "I almost forgot!" He took the small baggie out of his coat pocket and handed Bruce the bottle of pills.

"Looks like an antibiotic," the younger man said, raising an eyebrow.

"Yeah," said Frank, "I just need to know if that is all it is." Bruce nodded.

"Gotcha," he said, "I'll let you know."

"Thanks," replied Frank, heading out the door and back to the hospital. He was hoping Stephanie was well enough to answer a few questions.

Chapter 18

Frank walked out of the elevator on the second floor and immediately saw Brian. The nurse was standing at the end of the hall, talking to the officer by the door to Stephanie's room.

"Hi Brian," Frank smiled, then nodded to the officer. "Anything new?" he asked. The men exchanged a look, then turned back to Frank.

"Sir," began Officer Jamison, "I was just getting ready to call you..."his voice trailed off and he stared bleakly at the detective, his tongue moistening his lips. At that moment Frank caught movement behind them in the room.

A tall, thin young man in a suit was working with an orderly to lift a body bag onto a gurney. Frank looked at the empty bed, then back at Brian.

"She didn't make it," he said, answering Frank's unspoken question. "There was too much damage to her vital organs. She died about thirty minutes ago." His eyes were moist.

Frank looked at the two young men in front of him and realized it must be hard on them. Neither was a stranger to death, but this was a young, vibrant, woman their age, who had apparently been deliberately poisoned.

"There was nothing you could do," he said, giving them a half hearted smile. Maybe it would at least alleviate some of their discomfort.

They stood aside as the gurney passed through the door. All three watched silently as it was wheeled slowly down the hallway, and into the elevator. Stephanie's body would be taken down in a closed elevator to the back of the hospital, and transferred into the waiting hearse.

"Did she have any other visitors? Other than Ken?" he asked. They exchanged glances, then shook their heads back and forth.

"Negative, Sir," replied Jamison. No one while I was on duty, and the officer I relieved this morning said there were no visitors after you left yesterday."

"So, you have no next of kin listed?" he asked Brian.

"No Sir," shrugged the former linebacker, "we put in a call to her employer, but we have not heard back from them."

"Let me know if you find out anything else," Frank said. "I'd like a look at her personal belongings, and I want copies of the latest lab results."

"On it," said Brian, as he turned to walk down to the nurse's station.

Frank blew out a frustrated breath as he waited for Ken to be brought back to the interrogation room. He rubbed his hands over his face as he realized he was going to have to let the man go, and he had very few leads. Frank sat silently as Ken was led in and seated across from him.

"You have nothing on me!" Ken burst out. "You have to let me go; I need to go see Stephanie and explain I had nothing to do with hurting her!" Frank continued to stare at the young man.

"That's not going to happen," said Frank.

"You have no reason to keep me away from her!" Ken was flushed now, obviously agitated. Frank decided to go for it. He leaned towards Ken.

"Do you know her next of kin?" he said levelly.

"I haven't met her family yet," said Ken, "but after I convince her…" His voice trailed off and he sat perfectly still, not blinking. When he finally spoke, his voice quivered and he spoke so softly it was almost a whisper. "Why would you ask me that?" His face was pale and he began to shake. "She's okay, isn't she?"

"She died about an hour ago," said Frank. Ken shook his head back and forth rapidly, in denial. Tears welled up in his eyes and ran down his face. He lowered his head to the table and sat, sobbing.

"She was the only thing in my life that mattered," Ken said through his weeping. "And now she is gone," he whimpered. His wet eyes rose to meet Frank's gaze. "Get whoever did this, detective, please!" he pleaded. "She deserves at least that much." He buried his head in his arms again and wept hysterically.

Frank watched him for several more minutes, then decided the grief was real. "Release him when he's ready," Frank said to the officer outside as he walked away. He was tired and exasperated. He had two dead women, no real leads, and no next of kin for either of them.

Chapter 19

Frank opened the door to the office of "We do it Your Way" and heard subdued arguing. He looked at the smiling face at the desk in front of him and raised an eyebrow.

"Welcome to "We do it Your Way," smiled the young brunette. "Can I help you?" Frank stepped up to the desk and showed the Renaissance wench his badge. Her mouth fell open and she fidgeted nervously, glancing over her shoulder.

"I just started here this morning," she said, obviously flustered. "I don't know anything; I just needed a job."

"I'm not here to cause you trouble, uh, Celeste," Frank said, looking at her name badge. She visibly relaxed and he continued. "I'm here to talk to Chad or Nina." Celeste looked over her shoulder again.

"They're…busy right now," she whispered, her eyes big. She pointed to the hall, where the angry voices could still be heard, albeit more softly than he would have thought.

He leaned forward over the desk and smiled. "I'll just show myself back there," he said softly. "I'll tell them you tried to stop me." He winked and walked around the desk to the break room.

Frank found Nina and Chad red faced, with hands flying for punctuation, as their stage whispers filled the air between them.

"Can't you just keep your hands off the bimbos for even a week?" fumed Nina. "We are under investigation!"

"I never touched Stephanie!" hissed Chad.

"Oh, right, you expect me to believe it was only Ginger?" Nina snarled.

"No! I never…" began Chad, when he suddenly became aware of Frank standing in the doorway. Nina followed his eyes and they both stood, rooted to the spot, staring at him. Nina was the first to speak.

"I told Celeste we were not to be disturbed!" she snapped.

"She tried to stop me," lied Frank, but I am a lot bigger than she, and you know, there is this," he said, flashing his badge.

"What are you doing here, Detective?" asked Chad, portraying a much calmer front than Nina. "Is there something else we can help you with?" It was an unsuccessful attempt at composure. The moisture on his forehead and his clenched hands did not match his voice.

"Where were you the afternoon and evening someone poisoned

Stephanie?" Frank shot back. Chad straightened in surprise and took a step back.

"I was out of town on business," he stammered.

"Business my ass!" retorted Nina. Frank let the tension build before speaking again.

"What business would that be?" asked Frank.

"I had to recruit new employees," answered Chad, "with Ginger gone and Stephanie in the hospital…"

"Stephanie is dead," said Frank.

Chad registered shock as he staggered backward and dropped into a chair. He sat mute, his mouth open, staring at Frank. Nina gasped and felt for the other chair, then sank into it, her hands falling in her lap.

"When?" Chad finally managed. The color had drained from his face and his hands were shaking.

"About an hour and a half ago," said Frank, watching them both closely. They appeared to be genuinely stunned and sat silent. He let it play out and they turned their heads to look at each other. They both shook their heads no at the other. *Now isn't that interesting, Frank thought.* It was very revealing that they would check with each other for a cursory confirmation that each was innocent of that crime.

"Did she ever say anything?" asked Chad. Frank stared hard at him.

"Where were you yesterday, Mr. Roberts?"

"I told you, I was out of town looking for new employees." He looked at Frank, puzzled.

"Exactly where? Who did you talk to?" grilled Frank.

"Wait a minute, you don't think…"

"I think you better come with me," said Frank. "But first, Mrs. Roberts, I need phone numbers and addresses for the next of kin for both Ginger and Stephanie."

Nina snorted. "We don't keep that kind of information on our employees," she said sarcastically. "They aren't children," she finished, as she rolled her eyes. Frank stepped over to her and leaned into her face.

"They are somebody's children," he growled. "Now find me some information, and do it now, unless you want to do it from the station." His eyes did not waver from hers and she flushed as he continued to stare her down.

"I'll go see what I can find out right now," she said, rising and scooting around him as he stood back. She clomped down the hall and he turned his attention back to Chad.

"Let's go," said Frank, hooking a thumb towards the door.

"You have nothing on me!" Chad protested.

"Okay," said Frank, straddling a chair and folding his arms across the top. "Give me names and contact information." He held his tablet with the pencil poised to write, and stared at Chad. The man shifted in his chair and shot a glance at the doorway. He rubbed his hands on his thighs and wet his lips. He looked at Frank.

"Let's go to the station, okay?" he said. Frank did not move. "It'll be quieter there," implored Chad.

"Good idea," said Frank in mock agreement, standing and waving for Chad to walk ahead of him. Frank followed Chad down the short hall and through the office, noting the scared look on the face of the new employee and the angry visage on Nina's face. Nina had an open file in front of her on the desk.

"I'll be back as soon as I can," said Chad to Nina, who merely glared at him.

"Let me know as soon as you find any information that would help us contact next of kin," Frank said pointedly to Nina.

"Of course," she said primly, but her eyes shot daggers at both of the men. Frank nodded at Celeste to reassure her he had covered for her, then closed the door behind them.

Chapter 20

Chad walked towards the passenger side while Frank went around the front of the car and opened his door. He put a foot on the floor board, then stopped. Chad was standing beside the car, shifting back and forth and chewing on his lip.

"Get in the car, Chad," said Frank.

"Uh, well, I mean…" he fidgeted nervously and looked at Frank, then down at the ground, then back again.

"Get in now!" barked Frank.

"Front or back?" Chad blurted out. The corner of Frank's mouth twitched as he pretended to think about it for a minute.

"Front," he finally deadpanned.

"Thank you," Chad breathed, obviously relieved, as he opened the front door and lowered himself into the seat. He gave Frank a bleak smile and got no reaction.

Frank drove an unmarked detective car, and there was no grill between the front and back of the car. He would rather take his chances with someone beside him than behind him, but he wasn't about to tell Chad why he was in the front. He wanted him off balance; people spilled more secrets when they were unsure of themselves.

They drove in silence to the station, then walked inside. Frank led the way into the room and pointed to the chair beside his desk. Chad sank into the chair and began to drum his fingers on the desk. Frank sat down and stared first at his fingers, then at his face until Chad stopped.

"Start talking, Chad."

"Okay," he said, blowing out a long breath and rubbing his hands over his face. He hesitated, as if he were searching for the right words. "Nina can be…well, difficult," he began.

"Uh huh," said Frank, Coughing into his hand to hide the grin he could not help.

"So," Chad said with resignation, "I am not innocent." Frank held his breath. Chad leaned forward and put his elbows on his knees. He hung his head. He took a deep breath and then sat up straight. "I did something stupid with Ginger." Frank merely nodded. "But I didn't kill her, and I never did anything to hurt Stephanie!"

"Go on." Frank sat very still.

"Nina was really in Ginger's face one day." He ran his hand over the top of his head. "She was yelling at her and really saying some ugly things about Ginger being an orphan. Nina was red in the face and it was so awful. Ginger was crying and asking her to please stop." Chad shook his head. "Ginger was cowering in front of her and couldn't get away. Nina had her penned in and wouldn't let her leave. She kept bobbing back and forth to block Ginger." His face seemed like he was reliving the scene in his head. "It was cruel and I went over and told Nina to stop it. She actually hit me and told me it was none of my business!" He pulled on his lip with his teeth. "I had never seen Nina like that," he said to Frank.

"What did you do?" asked the detective.

"I stepped between Ginger and Nina, then I grabbed Ginger's arm and led her away from Nina."

"Where did you take her?"

"I put her in my car. Nina was screaming from the doorway and I told her to go take a shower and freshen up. I thought it might calm her down."

"Did you and Ginger go somewhere in your car?" asked Frank, still forming the relationship between Ginger and Chad in his head.

"Yes," Chad sighed. "She was really upset. She didn't want to go someplace public when she was crying, and we couldn't go to her place or mine because Nina knew where both those places were." He looked at Frank with sadness. "I made a really big mistake."

"Go on," encouraged Frank, his senses sharpening.

"I took her to a cheap motel and got her a room." Chad wiped at his eyes and shook his head. "How could I be so dumb!"

"So, you did have a relationship with Ginger?" questioned the detective. Chad stared at him for a few minutes, not comprehending.

"What?" he acted like he didn't understand the question. Then his eyes got big. "No! No, you got it all wrong!" he protested. "Ginger and I didn't do…you know, anything wrong! Geez! No, she was like my kid sister!" He stood and paced in front of the desk. "We just talked! I mean, I held her for a few minutes when she was really crying hard, but it wasn't, like, oh that's just nasty!"He made a face and gave Frank an accusatory look.

"So, let me get this straight," said Frank, standing and walking around the desk. He stood in front of Chad. "Nina was berating Ginger and you rescued her. Then you took her to a motel room, where nothing happened?" His eyes were hard as he held Chad in his sights.

"That's right!" Chad declared with determination, "I never touched her in an inappropriate way!" His mouth was set in a grim line and he stood, hands on hips, challenging Frank to question his story.

"You said you made a big mistake," Frank repeated, and let the statement hang in the air between them.

"Damn it!" said Chad, sitting down hard. He looked up at Frank in frustration. "Don't you get it?" Frank towered over him, rock still. "I rented a cheap motel room and took Ginger there! I left for awhile and she fell asleep, then I came back with some food."

"And?" snapped Frank, his patience wearing thin.

"And nothing! We ate dinner together and I left her there to spend the night where she could really get some rest without being disturbed."

"You left her there?"

"Yes! Alone!" he growled. "But Nina saw the bill when it came and all hell broke loose. She wouldn't believe we didn't do anything wrong." Chad bent forward and covered his face with his hands, rocking back and forth. "THAT was my big mistake!" Frank sat on the edge of his desk, watching Chad.

"What about being out of town when Stephanie was poisoned?"

"Yeah, I was at a temp agency in Carson City, looking for some talent – someone who could dress up, carry a tune, be good with kids. You know, basic stuff."

"Can anyone verify that?"

"Yeah," said Chad, reaching into his pocket for his wallet. He extracted a card and handed it to Frank. "Give this lady a call. This is where I found Celeste." Frank took the card and studied it while Chad gave the floor his attention.

"Why didn't you just tell me this back at the office?" asked Frank.

"Are you kidding?" Chad smiled weakly. "I knew we would get around to talking about Ginger and Stephanie, and I did not want to go through all that again." He raised an eyebrow at Frank. "Would you?" he continued.

Frank deliberated for a few minutes, then smiled. "No, probably not," he agreed, and Chad smiled back. He sighed and Chad looked up from his seat. "You're free to go, Chad," he said.

"Thank you," he said. "You have to believe me, detective." His eyes were moist. "I wouldn't hurt those girls." He started towards the door and was almost through it when Frank remembered something.

"Chad?"

"Yes," said Chad, turning back to face him.

"You said you told Nina to take a shower and freshen up." Frank was watching his face.

"Yeah, that's right," he said.

"Why would you say that to her?" the detective asked, narrowing his eyes.

"Because sometimes she sits in that damn Jacuzzi so long, she has to rush when she gets out so she can get to work." He wrinkled his nose. "She doesn't shower and she smells like bleach!"

Chapter 21

Frank put in a call to Nina while Chad was on his way back to the office.

"We do it Your Way, how can I help you?" oozed Nina on the other end of the line. Frank was surprised he didn't have to go through Celeste; that Nina had answered the phone herself.

"Detective Riley, Mrs. Roberts. Do you have any of that contact information for me yet?" he said evenly.

"Oh, I am so sorry, detective," she said too sweetly, "I was just about to call you." He knew she was lying, and enjoying trying to push his buttons. "It is such a shame, we have nothing on either young woman."

"Not even a friend listed?" he said, controlling his disgust as he clenched his jaw.

"Sadly, no," she sighed. "We may need to take your advice and add that request to our application," she said, as if she just thought of the idea. Frank had even more sympathy for Chad at this moment.

"Let me know if you come up with anyone," he said.

"Oh, of course, detective!" Her agreement was as fake as a three dollar bill, but he could do nothing about it right now.

Frank hung up the phone and stared at it, as if it held the answer he needed, but it wouldn't talk. Suddenly, he stood. Of course! He walked down the hall to the evidence room and stood in front of Noah.

"Hey Noah, can I see the personal belongings for Ginger Snapper and Stephanie Evers, please?" The young man flipped the book around for Frank to sign as he stood.

"Sure, Frank, give me a second." He walked back through the gate to the room and quickly came back with two boxes.

Frank opened the lid and immediately saw what he was seeking. He picked up Ginger's phone and turned it on, but it was too weak. He opened the other box and found Stephanie's phone in the same condition.

"Anyway you can charge these up for me?" he asked.

"Sure! Both of those are pretty new. I am sure we have chargers for them. He took the phones and walked over to a small table against the wall, where a bank of outlets and cords were plugged in. He selected two and fit the ends into the receptacles on the phones. The beep told them they were charging. Noah looked at each phone, then back at Frank.

"Should be ready in fifteen or twenty minutes," he said.

"Thanks, I'll be back," said Frank. He walked out the door and over to the ME building.

Chapter 22

Frank opened the door and caught Sierra standing by Bruce's desk, in conversation with the young assistant.

"Good morning," he said to both of them, but was looking at Sierra to gauge her reaction. They had not spoken since he had crossed the line between business and personal.

"Detective," she said coolly, "something we can help you with?"

"How are you?" he smiled in a lame attempt to repair his mistake.

"Fine, thank you, but we have a lot of work to do," she answered. "If you don't need me, I'll leave you in the capable hands of Bruce." She hesitated only a second, waiting for an answer, then turned away.

Bruce arched an eyebrow at Frank, then looked at Sierra's retreating back as she quickly walked away. "Wow!" he whispered, giving Frank a quizzical look. "What did you do?" His eyes were wide as he stood, hands on hips, waiting.

"Something really stupid," sighed Frank.

"I'm not sure I even want to know," Bruce groaned.

"Oh yeah, I really went for it. Now I am not sure how to get back from the 'dark side'," he smiled wryly.

"Lots of the cops have hit on her, I mean, she is a very attractive woman and single," said Bruce. "But she has not been that frosty to any of them." He examined Frank's face. "Okay, spill it, what did you do?"

Frank sat down and rubbed his hand over his chin. He looked at the other man. "One night I was sitting in my car, thinking over the day, before I went home. I saw Sierra come out of the building. She was hunched over as she walked, her arms folded across her body." Bruce nodded expectantly. "I could swear I saw her wipe at her eyes, like she was crying. She didn't see me." He looked at Bruce. "I couldn't help myself – you know, it's the cop thing." He sighed.

"Oh boy, this sounds bad," said Bruce, shaking his head. "Keep talking."

"The other day I brought in muffins and coffee to pick her brain about the evidence on the Snapper and Devers cases." Frank shrugged his shoulders in resignation.

"Uh huh," Bruce said with apprehension clearly in his voice. He sat back in his chair and crossed his arms across his chest, eyebrows raised in expectation.

"It was going great, she was helpful with her insights and she actually seemed relaxed." He ran a hand over his hair. "So, I asked her if she was okay and I told her I thought I saw her crying that night," he blurted out all at once.

"You didn't!" Bruce sat forward in his chair and looked at Frank in disbelief.

"Oh yeah, I did." Frank clenched and unclenched his hands. "I am a first class idiot." Bruce said nothing and Frank turned to look at him. The younger man was staring at a file on the desk and his right leg was jumping up and down like he was keeping beat to some music only he could hear. "Bruce?"

"The truth is," said Bruce slowly, bringing his gaze back up, "I am pretty sure I have caught her crying once or twice too." Silence sat between them like a pile of dead fish that had sat in the sun for days. Neither of them wanted to touch it; they just stared at each other.

"Any idea what is going on?" asked Frank. Bruce shook his head and spread his hands in the air.

"Not a clue. She doesn't talk about her personal life and there are no pictures anywhere on her desk. "

"Well, I guess it isn't our business, but…let me know if you see or hear anything that makes you think she is in any danger, okay?" Frank felt helpless, but he couldn't poke around in her personal life without a damn good reason.

"Absolutely," said Bruce, drawing himself up straight. "So. What brings you to our fine establishment?" he asked, changing the subject.

"Anything funny on the bottle of pills from Ken's locker, or the water bottle belonging to Stephanie?" he asked. This case was eating at him; he needed the pieces to fall into place. He had an uneasy feeling that this was not the end of the murders.

"Yeah," said Bruce, turning to his computer and clicking on a file. The printer whirred and he handed Frank the pages that printed out. "Stephanie was poisoned with a high grade pesticide containing large amounts of arsenic."

"Arsenic! Then it was no accident," responded Frank.

"No," said Bruce. "It had to be deliberate."

"What about the pills from Ken's locker? Anything?"

"Here's where it gets really interesting," said Bruce. "One of the capsules was pure arsenic."

" Someone deliberately replaced the antibiotic?" exclaimed Frank.

"Looks that way," said Bruce. Frank sat in deep thought for a few moments. "That means the only reason Ken isn't dead too is because he didn't take all the antibiotic." Bruce added. Frank brought his eyes up to meet Bruce's gaze.

"Unless he did it himself to throw me off." Frank said flatly. "Thanks, Bruce," said Frank, standing and walking towards the door. "Catch you later!"

Chapter 23

Frank slowly sauntered back to the department with his head down and his hands in his pockets. The details of the case were popping around his brain like an out of control ping pong ball. He rubbed his hands over his head and tugged at an ear.

"Damn, I miss having Jack to brain storm with me!" he said, opening the door and continuing towards Noah's desk.

"Ready for you!" offered Noah, standing and reaching behind his desk. He disconnected the phones from their chargers and held them out to Frank.

"Thanks, Noah," said Frank, signing the register and waving the phones in the air as he walked back to his desk.   Frank started through the short address book on Ginger's phone and began calling the names. The Clancy's and Jim Munson were the only live voices that answered his entreaty, and the Clancy's had no names or numbers for him. Jim Munson gave him a name from Ginger's application and Frank called, but no one answered. He left messages at all the numbers, except for one that had been disconnected. It didn't take long; apparently Ginger did not have a lot of friends, and most of the numbers had been in other states.

Next, he called the numbers in Stephanie's phone. On the third number he reached a woman who responded to his identification with apprehension.

"I'm April Morgan, and Stephanie Devers is my sister, detective. Is she alright?"

"I'm afraid not, Ms. Morgan," said Frank. "Is there anyone there with you?" He hated this part of his job. People going happily through their lives, and suddenly he calls and their world goes dark and cold.

"Yes, my husband is here, but you're scaring me detective. Is my sister alright?" He could hear the trembling in her voice.

"Could you get your husband please, M'am?" Frank asked calmly.

"Sam!" he heard April yell. Her tone was frantic; she was frightened. "Tell me what is going on!" Her voice was breaking now.

"Stephanie is dead, Mrs. Morgan."

Absolute silence hung on the other end of the line for several seconds. He could just about picture what was happening; shock, denial, questions, then the emotion hits.

"My sister?" she breathed. "Not my sister! Oh God, oh God, no!" The woman was sobbing now, wailing in disbelief. The phone clattered against a hard object, probably a counter or a table, like it had been dropped. Frank heard another voice in the background.

"April? April, honey, what is it?" said a man.

"Stephanie! Stephanie's dead, Sam! She's dead!" April wailed. Frank waited patiently. He heard the phone being fumbled.

"This is Sam Morgan, April's husband, who is this?" The man was demanding, and Frank understood. His wife was hurting and Frank was the cause, in Sam's eyes. Sam was kicking into protector mode.

"Mr. Morgan, this is Detective Frank Riley of the South Lake Tahoe Police Department. I am afraid I had to give your wife some bad news." He stopped, knowing the questions needed to be asked.

"Stephanie is...really...gone?" Sam asked, the reality beginning to sink in.

"Yes, I am sorry to say she passed away yesterday. We have been trying to find her next of kin."

"How? She was so young!"

"I'm sorry, sir, it is an open investigation. It is too early to be certain of the cause of death." He knew it was an unsatisfactory answer.

"Detective, please. I have to tell my wife something! Was it an accident?" pleaded Sam.

Frank hesitated. "It would appear your sister-in-law was poisoned, but we don't have all the information yet." Frank steeled himself for the angry burst.

"That's crazy! What do you mean, poisoned? Was it accidental, or...?" Frank could almost hear the wheels turning in the man's mind. He was not surprised when Sam's tone became confrontational. 'Who would do such a thing? I'll kill the son of a bitch!" Frank could hear April weeping hysterically in the background.

"Mr. Morgan, we don't have a lot of details yet. I will keep you informed, I promise," offered Frank. It never seemed like it was enough. There was more silence, but Frank knew Sam had not hung up the phone. He could still hear April crying.

"Where," began Sam, then cleared his throat. "Where can we, uh...," he stopped, unable to ask the question.

"Her body is still at the morgue here. If you are coming in, please let me know and I will make arrangements for you to claim the body." Frank's stomach turned sour. It never got easier. This was one of the worst times of their life, and the pain was so intense at the point he had to speak to them. He gave Sam Morgan his phone number.

"Thank you, detective. I should go now, and see to my wife, but we will be in touch." The voice was soft now, grief was pulling the man down.

Frank dropped the phone back in its cradle and sat, staring at the file on the desk. He drummed his fingers on the desk, then abruptly stood and headed for the parking lot.

Chapter 24

Frank drove slowly through the mostly barren neighborhood. It had been ten years since the Angora Fire had ravaged the vegetation and left burned rubble in place of homes. Lives had been devastated, personal treasures and family heirlooms lost forever, and many of the people had simply taken the insurance money and moved away. It was too painful to stay, and many were haunted by the vision of a recurrence some day . The land was slow to regenerate, and many of the black skeletons of trees still stood, giving the area a ghastly appearance.

He passed through the worst of it, and turned up a slight hill to where a few houses had survived the inferno. It had been a long time since he had driven down this street. He slowed and searched the addresses and house fronts as he crawled along, looking for the sea green stucco with dark green trim. It had been awhile, but he was sure he would recognize the house.

"Ah!" he said, pulling to the curb in front of a neatly kept, slightly brown lawn. He got out and walked up the empty driveway. Stepping up on the small stoop in front of the door, he knocked. He heard footsteps coming slowly towards the door and smiled in anticipation.

But the man who answered the door was not his friend, Jack Hogan. His smile faded as he took in the man that stood on the other side of the door way. Instead of the hearty, jovial man that had been the Medical Examiner, a shrunken, thin man with pale skin stood staring back at him. His friend Jack had a full head of salt and pepper hair and this man was completely bald. Where Jack had been vibrant, this man was leaning on a walker.

"I'm sorry, " Frank stammered, "I was looking for my old friend, Jack Hogan."

"Frank Riley, you son of a sea biscuit, I wondered when you would miss me and show up at my door!" The man grinned, and Frank caught the glimmer of humor that went with the smile.

"Jack?" Frank said in disbelief. What had happened to his friend? He did not recognize him.

"Come in, before the neighbors start to talk," said Jack. He began to shuffle back to the living area, leaving Frank to follow and push the door shut. He pushed the walker in front of him, and Frank noticed the front of the walker had wheels. Jack lowered himself carefully into a worn brown leather easy chair, and looked at Frank.

"Want a beer?" he asked Frank. "I'll let you get it yourself; right there in the fridge in the kitchen." Jack was breathing hard and a light shimmer of moisture shone on his forehead.

"I don't want to be any trouble," said Frank, still at a loss to understand what had happened to his colleague.

"Oh for heaven's sake, Frank, I'm not dead yet!" wheezed Jack. "Get yourself a beer and park it! I have someone bring them in for me every week. I even have one myself once in awhile!"

"Do you want one?"asked Frank, stepping towards the opening onto the kitchen.

"Nah, right now, one beer would put me to sleep and you just got here!"

Frank opened the refrigerator and retrieved a beer. The fridge was clean, and stocked mostly with nutrition drinks, juices, and boxes of soup. He popped the top on the beer, took a long swig, and walked back to the living room. He sat down opposite Jack and was surprised to hear the man begin to laugh, a brittle sound that ended with a cough.

"Jesus, Mary, and Joseph, Frank Riley," he chuckled. "I'm the one that is sick and you look like death warmed over twice!" He cocked his head at Frank. "I've got cancer, Frank, now for the love of God, smile! I'm beginning to think I died and don't know it yet, by the look on your face!"

Frank laughed in spite of himself. The glint in Jack's eyes did not match his physical appearance. The spirit in the man was still strong, and it relaxed Frank to see the old friend inside the frail body.

"That's more like it!" he grinned.

"It's good to see you, Jack," said Frank.

"It's good to be seen," chortled Jack.

"I'm sorry, Jack, I guess I got busy and then one day I came to work and you weren't there. You just disappeared. Even Bruce wouldn't say anything when I asked him."

Jack nodded. "Good man, that Bruce," he said. He looked at Frank. "I wanted it that way." His eyes were level and clear as he stared at Frank.

"I couldn't figure it out. There was no retirement party, nothing, you were just gone!"

"I wanted it that way," Jack repeated. Everyone knew I was

talking about retiring. Then one day I went in for a checkup. Told the doc I was tired all the time. He did some blood work, and told me I had cancer."

"Why didn't you let us help?" asked Frank.

"Help with what? You an oncologist now?" He chuckled again. "You always were a smart one, Frankie, but how could you have helped?" Jack was the only one who ever got away with calling him Frankie.

"There must have been something I could have done," protested Frank. He took another swig of the beer, still feeling helpless.

"Eh!" exclaimed Jack, feebly swiping at the air. "Listen, I got a diagnosis of Hodgkin Lymphoma. We caught it early and the survival rate is good." He studied Frank's face, which showed the powerless concern he had seen on most of his visitors. Not that there were many; he was fighting this battle privately. "Susie died a decade ago, and the house is paid for. I had enough money to hire people to do what I needed," Jack said decisively.

"I would have gone with you to treatment," began Frank. "I hate the idea of you going through this alone." He looked at Jack and was surprised at the knot in his throat.

"I know," said Jack. "But it was time for me to retire, and then I got sick. The doc said I had a good chance of beating this, if I took care of myself during the treatment." He looked at a picture still sitting on the table beside him. It was him and Susie, on the day they got married. "I figured if I made it, I could look up my friends. And if I didn't, well, Susie would be waiting for me."

"How many more treatments do you have?" asked Frank carefully. He wanted to know, but he didn't want to make it harder for Jack.

"One. Next week," he said. Frank held his face very still and Jack grinned. He leaned forward and poked his hand in Frank's direction. "It's okay, Frankie. The doc says it looks good. Really!" He grinned and Frank exhaled the breath he didn't realize he had been holding in.

"Now," Jack said, "you didn't look me up just to see how I am doing. What's on your mind?"

"I don't know…," shrugged Frank.

"The hell you say! I need something to put my brain cells to work! Talk to me!"

Frank nodded and started to lay out the case to the best medical examiner he had ever known.

Chapter 25

Frank was only a few sentences into explaining the case when Jack held up a hand, palm out. He stood slowly and looked at Frank, an impish grin on his face.

"Let's step into my office," he said with a twinkle in his eye. He moved slowly, but with determination, to a hallway on the opposite side of the living room from the kitchen.

The first door on the right of the hall was shut, the only closed door in the hall, Frank noted. Jack turned the handle and gave the door a push, then wobbled inside the room to a comfortable desk chair. As he sat, he pointed to a small office waiting room style chair against one wall.

"Pull that chair over here and have a seat, although it won't be for long!" smiled Jack.

Frank stood just inside the room for a few seconds, staring at one whole wall of whiteboard and multi-colored sticky notes. He pulled the chair over closer to Jack, as directed, but just as he started to sit, Jack spoke.

"Go on over to the board and take down all those notes," he directed. Frank did as he was told. "Just stack them on top of each other and put them on top of that file cabinet, " Jack said. "My last case before I retired, "he quipped.

"This is where you laid out your cases?" Frank said with surprise, looking at a few of the notes as he removed them. "I thought you did your work at the ME building offices."

"Heck no! Too many interruptions, like detectives coming in and asking questions!" he chortled as Frank turned red and managed a limp smile. "Old technique; take the details one at a time and stick them in the categories." He pointed to the titles on the top of the whiteboard. "Are they a suspect? Is it an unusual detail? Something that doesn't seem to fit, but feels important? Miscellaneous for everything that doesn't fit in another place, at least until the case is solved."

"Seeing it all laid out in front of you could help!" said Frank. "That's my problem right now! All these details banging around in my head, but some don't make sense. Then I feel like there is something I am missing." He looked at Jack. "It's driving me crazy!" The older man laughed.

"Ok, now open that drawer right there, the top one," he pointed to a small desk against the wall. Frank opened it and saw dozens of small pads of different colored sticky post it notes.

"You must have done a lot of work here at home!" exclaimed Frank.

"Nearly every night, especially after Susie died, I would sit in here for an hour or two, just staring at my notes. Sometimes I'd move one or two around. They would 'talk' to me," he sighed. He sat still for a few minutes, and Frank waited. Then he lifted his head and gave Frank a knowing look. "Grab a bunch of those note pads and some of those dry erase markers too," said Jack. "Lay them out on the little TV tray there, under the board."

Frank did as he was told, and felt a growing excitement. He was going to put his case in front of one of the most brilliant ME's in the business, and two sets of eyes were going to examine all the details. For the first time since the case began, he felt hope that a resolution would come soon.

"Okay, now start with the victims," said Jack. "Pick a different color for each one." He watched as Frank wrote Ginger on one sheet and Stephanie on another and stuck them on the board.

"They both worked for the same company," said Frank, putting two colored sticky notes under the column that listed what they had in common. "Ginger had no family, but Stephanie did. He placed those notes under differences.

"Cause of death?" asked Jack, his eyes on the board.

" Poison," decided Frank. "Different types, but still poison." He put another of the same color under each name.

"Explain," said Jack.

"Ginger was poisoned with chlorine," said Frank, "she was allergic to the substance, so I would say she was poisoned." Jack nodded in agreement. "And, her inhaler was tampered with." He twisted his mouth in a grimace. "Ginger's murder was more complicated than Stephanie's."

"Hmmm. Why?" muttered Jack. "Put that up there under the allergy to chlorine," said Jack. "What about Stephanie?"

"Straight poison. Arsenic in her water bottle." Frank slapped a sticky note on the board.

"Deliberate, fast, no mistakes likely," said Jack, rubbing his chin. Both men contemplated the board in silence, eyes moving over the details. "Anyone you like for these murders?"

"My suspects are numerous, and have me really confused," sighed Frank. "Both were essentially poisoned, but they feel different, somehow."

"Put them up, and let's see if we can shake something loose." Jack's voice was softer, and Frank turned his head to look at his old friend. Jack sat back in his chair and closed his eyes for a moment.

"Jack, I am wearing you out, I should go," said Frank. He did not want to go, but his old friend suddenly looked tired.

"Don't you dare leave now!" Jack's eyes snapped open and he glared at Frank. "Just a little twinge; they happen! I haven't felt this energized in months!" He sat forward again. "Now, let's see those suspects!"

Frank spent another second studying the face of his friend, then satisfied the man was truly alright, turned back to the board. "Nina Roberts is high on my list of suspects, but I just don't like the woman, so I need to make sure that is not coloring my judgment." He slapped a note on the board under Suspects.

"Okay, put them all up, and then we will talk about them," said Jack, his eyes scanning the board nonstop.

"Then there is Chad Roberts, Nina's husband." He added another sticky note to the board. He scribbled on another note. "Ken is an employee at the company, and seems to have been infatuated with Stephanie." Frank stuck that note up as well.

"Now," said Jack, "who else is in the picture, but not yet considered a suspect." Frank peered sharply at the old man. He had been so focused on those three, he had not yet allowed himself to think of the non obvious. He thought for a moment.

"Jim Munson is the owner and manager of the apartment complex where Ginger lived. Then we have the Clancy's," said Frank slowly, thinking.

"Anyone else?" prompted Jack.

"There is another employee named Michelle, and a new one named Celeste." Frank studied the board as he put up their names. "That's all I've got."

"Now, tell me what you have, think, and feel about each one," said Jack. "Anything and everything; like free writing, just say what comes into your head." Frank stared silently at the board, then looked at Jack and nodded.

"First, Celeste has not been there long enough to know anyone. She is from out of town." He moved her note to the end of the board, under "Miscellaneous." He chewed on his lip. "I just don't think the Clanceys had the physical strength to get to Ginger, and my gut doesn't see them for this. Their grief was genuine, and they had no motive." He moved their sticky note as well. "Jim Munson seemed to really like Ginger, and he had no real motive that I can see. He had access, but I don't have anything that points to him. As far as I know, he didn't even know Stephanie."

"Sit down for a minute," suggested Jack. Frank obeyed and they sat staring at the white expanse dotted with colorful squares of paper. "Get yourself another beer, and bring me one of those nutrition things from the refrigerator while you're at it," Jack said.

Frank stood, and once more went to the kitchen. He liked laying out the case, and he had to admit, Jack had a little color in his cheeks now. He didn't want to wear his friend down; he needed to be careful. He retrieved the drinks and walked back in the room. Jack's eyes were roving over the board.

"Tell me about Nina," he said to Frank.

"Well, she is abrasive and nasty to just about everyone." He blew out a breath. "Has a little jealous streak, too, I think. I don't like her as a person, but I am not sure she killed anyone." He rubbed his chin. "But her husband said something that is nagging at me."

"Uh huh," Jack responded.

"He said that sometimes Nina spends so much time in her Jacuzzi, she rushes to work without showering, and she smells like bleach."

"Bleach? As in chlorine bleach?" Jack said with interest.

"Yeah, that's what clicked with me too," replied Frank. "But how does Stephanie play into Nina being the killer?"

"There is nothing to tie them together?" asked Jack.

"I searched the office and found nothing. That's where Ken came in," said Frank, gesturing towards the board. "He filled Stephanie's water bottle for her just before she was killed."

"Could he have slipped some poison in while he filled it?" asked Jack.

Frank shook his head. "The water bottle was on Stephanie's desk and I was standing right there when he filled it for her. It would have been tough to pull off." He leaned forward. "There's something else.

Ken had a prescription in his locker when I searched it. I had Bruce check it out."

"Did he find anything?"

"Yes," Frank nodded, "one of the capsules was pure arsenic."

"So, he either set it up to look like he could have been a victim, or he was intended to be one." Jack surveyed the board again. "Tell me about Michelle."

"She's an employee, " he shrugged. "The first time I saw her, she was arguing with Chad about Nina. Then she snapped at Ken on her way out, and that's all I have on her. Nothing jumped out in her background check."

"Did you hear any of the argument she had with Chad about Nina?"

"From what I heard, Michelle was unhappy with Nina," said Frank. "I heard her tell Chad to 'check his wife,' and then she stormed out of the office."

"Hmm. Sounds like Michelle had issues with Nina, but no one else. What about Chad?"

"Chad seems like he just wants everybody to be happy. Tough order with his wife!" Frank laughed. "He did get between Nina and Ginger one day."

"Really. Now that's interesting," said Jack. "Why?"

"Nina was yelling at Ginger and had her penned in a corner. Chad told her to stop, Nina didn't, and Chad pulled Ginger away and took her to a motel room."

"Jealousy for motive?" asked Jack, raising what eyebrows he had left.

"Chad swears nothing happened, that he looked at Ginger as a kid sister. But Nina does seem to be the type that really doesn't like her husband, but doesn't want anyone else to give him any attention."

"Anybody else have a motive?' asked Jack.

"No, not that I have found."

"Well, it's pretty thin, Frank," said Jack,

"I know. And worse, I have this awful feeling it isn't over yet." His phone vibrated in his pocket and he pulled it out. "Riley," he answered. He listened as he looked at Jack. "I'll be there to meet them," he said, then disconnected the call.

"Duty calls," grinned Jack.

"Yeah, Stephanie's relatives are on their way in and I promised I would meet them to take them to the morgue."He stood and so did Jack. Frank resisted the impulse to put his arm under the older man's elbow and assist him. He knew Jack would not like that.

Frank followed Jack, but as he started to pull the door to the room shut, Jack stopped him. "Leave it, Frankie," the man said. "I think I'll go back in there later and see if anything pops out at me." His eyes were droopy, and Frank could see he was fatigued, but he also saw a fresh glimmer in Jack's eyes.

They walked to the front door and Frank turned as he stepped through. "It was good to see you," said Frank.

"Likewise," smiled Jack. Frank turned to walk down the path when he heard the soft voice behind him. "Frank?"

"Yes, Jack?"

"Come back some time soon."

"I'd like that," said Frank. He hesitated only a second, then added "it really helps to have a sharp mind on the case."

"Make that TWO sharp minds," said Jack, with emphasis. Both men were smiling as Frank got in his car.

Chapter 26

At the station, Frank called over to let Bruce know Stephanie's sister was on the way to identify and claim the body.

"Medical Examiner's office, Dr. O'Malley speaking," said Sierra.

"Oh," said Frank with surprise, "I thought I dialed Bruce." It was silly, he knew, but he was not prepared for Sierra to answer the phone.

"Bruce is out today, may I help you?" she said.

"I'm sorry, Sierra, this is Frank Riley, how are you?" He was feeling childish for not identifying himself.

"With Bruce out, I am busier than ever, what can I do for you?" she repeated. All business, he noted.

"April Morgan and her husband Sam, are on their way in to identify and claim the body of Stephanie Devers. April is the sister of the victim." Silence. "I told her I would bring them over when they got here," he continued.

"How nice of you." He couldn't tell if that was meant to be sarcastic or a compliment. "I'll be ready." She hung up.

He hung up on his end and rubbed his hands over his face. He missed the old ME even more now. He wondered if he would ever be able to repair the damage he had done with Dr. O'Malley, and establish some kind of solid working relationship, like he had with Jack.

He turned on the computer while he was waiting and opened the case file. He began to reread the backgrounds on the employees at We do it Your Way. He still wanted to know why Nina Roberts had a closed juvenile file, but he kept hitting dead ends in the court system.

A sudden realization jumped out at him; he had missed it the first time through! Both Ken and Ginger had gone to the same high school. Why hadn't Ken mentioned that little detail? Did they know each other in high school? He hit a few more tabs, and sat back in his chair. They graduated in the same year, with a class of five hundred. It was possible they did not know each other, but he definitely had more questions for Ken.

His desk phone rang and he picked it up on the second ring. Stephanie's sister was here. He stood, took a deep breath, and walked out to reception. A tall, dark haired man of about thirty-five stood in the small room, with his arm around the waist of a blond woman with red rimmed eyes. It was easy to see the resemblance between her and Stephanie. He stepped through the glass door into the lobby and put his hand out.

"I'm Detective Frank Riley," he said, shaking hands with the man.

"I'm Sam Morgan, and this is my wife, April, Stephanie's sister." At the mention of her sister's name, April caught her breath. She took his hand in a listless hand shake and Frank noted the dullness in her eyes. It would not surprise him if she had been given some type of light sedative. Sometimes people had to deal with the grief a little at a time.

"Thank you for coming in," Frank said. It never sounded right to his ears, but it was some acknowledgement of the effort it took for the families to come to claim their loved ones. "Shall we go?" He had learned there was nothing to be gained by dragging it out. Most people just wanted to get it over with, and then go somewhere they could be alone with their pain.

They walked out the door to the ME building. Frank noted Sam kept his arm around his wife, half supporting her as she tottered on short heels. He opened the door for them and saw them hesitate a split second before crossing the threshold. They all knew lives would change forever with the finality that lay inside the cold, concrete building.

Sierra stood at the desk, with a solemn smile at the ready. She scanned their faces, then briefly shifted her eyes to Frank. Her eyes on the couple again, she stepped forward to meet them.

"I'm Doctor Sierra O'Malley," she said gently. "May I get you some water?" Both Sam and April declined. She studied them carefully. "It is not required that you see the body, so please know you don't have to do this if it is too much." She looked at Frank, and he saw the request in her eyes. He stepped forward.

"We have identified her through DNA testing," he said. "We already have a positive identification, so we can just make arrangements here for you to claim the body, if you would like." April and Sam exchanged a long look.

"I can do it, if you want, sweetheart," said Sam gently, holding both of April's hands in his. She wavered, then a resolute look came across her face.

"No, I need to do this for Stephanie," said April with false bravado. Sierra stood for a moment, as if waiting for April to change her mind. She checked Sam's expression, then turned.

"This way, please," she said, walking slowly down the hall next to them. Frank walked behind them, then stepped forward and pushed the button as they stopped in front of the elevator. The doors opened, and the four stepped inside.

No one said a word as the elevator descended to the basement level. Frank could hear April's ragged breathing and looked over her head at Sierra, who met his eyes. He read real concern in the ME's eyes. This was hard for her too, he realized.

When they stepped out of the elevator, Sierra moved in front of the couple. Gently, she touched April's arm. April raised her face to meet Sierra's eyes, and the two women stood, for a moment, sharing unspoken thoughts. April nodded and they turned towards the double lab doors.

Frank stepped forward again and held the door for all of them to move through. The drop in temperature assailed them immediately. April shivered like icy sleet had just unexpectedly hit the back of her neck.

"Honey?" asked Sam, as he stood even closer and gripped her tighter. April dissolved as if her spine had suddenly melted and Sam put both arms around her and pulled her tight against his chest.

"I caaann't, she stammered through tears. I'm sorry, I just can't see her like that."

"It's okay, baby, it's okay." Sam stroked her hair and rocked her softly side to side.

Frank and Sierra stood, waiting and watching. The pain in the room was palpable, and wrapped them all in its grip. They knew there was no rushing the grief; they were there to help in any way they could.

"Will you?" April asked Sam. "I can't, but I need..." her voice trailed off. Sam looked into her eyes and smiled a sad smile.

"Of course, sweetheart." Sam looked at Frank, and the detective stepped forward and accepted April from her husband's arms. He moved her so her back was to the cold lockers, to shield her from the sight of the corpse. He stiffened slightly when she fell against his chest, but he couldn't bring himself to push her away. He put his hands lightly on her arms in case she collapsed.

Sam took a deep breath and turned to Sierra, who pulled open the door of a cold locker and slid out the table. Sierra shot Frank a look.

There was always the chance that Sam would pass out when he saw the body. Frank shifted his eyes to the chair beside him and then back to Sierra and nodded. He would watch, and if Sierra signaled, he would set April in the chair and be at Sam's side the instant he showed any sign of wavering.

Sierra met Sam's eyes and he dipped his chin. She slid the sheet back from Stephanie's head and Sam gasped, then grabbed the table with both hands. He closed his eyes and put his head down for a brief few seconds, while Sierra watched him carefully. He stood up straight and looked Sierra in the eyes.

"Yes," he said, a tear rolling down one cheek. "That's Stephanie." April made a whimpering sound, and Sam moved quickly to her and took her in his arms again. Sierra covered the corpse and rolled it back into the locker. She closed the door and came towards them.

Frank opened the door to the hall and held it while they all went through. They went back upstairs and sat down at Bruce's desk, where they completed the paperwork for the body to be moved.

"Thank you, Doctor O'Malley. Thank you, Detective Riley," said Sam, while April bobbed her head up and down. "We appreciate your help." He hesitated.

"I'll keep you informed of the progress on the case," said Frank.

Sam's tears had been replaced by a new emotion. "Just get the bastard that did this, detective. Please." April emitted a sob at his words, and buried her face in her husband's chest.

"I will do my best," answered Frank. He meant what he said. He wanted the person who had snuffed out the lives of these two young women.

Sierra and Frank watched as Sam led his wife out to the parking lot. He heard the woman at his side sigh, and turned towards her. He was surprised to see a tear rolling down her cheek. Sierra seemed to be oblivious to his presence as she stood staring out the door. He waited.

Suddenly, she jerked her head up and looked at him as if she had not realized he was still there. She wiped her tears away and looked slightly disoriented.

"Sometimes the young ones get to me," she said distractedly.

"We have a tough job," he answered. "It gets to all of us sometimes." He had a strong urge to take her in his arms and just hold her, but he didn't. He would not cross that line again.

"It's so hard...," she started to say something, then stopped. "Thank you for your help, Frank," she said meeting his eyes. You were very kind to them."

"I'm glad I could help," he said, noting she used his first name. Was there more to this than he knew?

She nodded, and turned to walk away, then stopped. She locked eyes with him and he saw pain still lingering. "I'm glad you were here," she said, then briskly walked away.

He watched her for a few moments, then went back to his desk. He had made progress with Sierra; she was speaking to him again and called him by his first name. But there was definitely something going on, and he wished to hell he knew what it was.

Chapter 27

The next morning, Frank glued himself to his computer, searching through the background info for Nina and Ken. He managed to find Ken's school records and called the district office, looking for some of Ken's old teachers.

One of them was still teaching, and the secretary at the office gave Frank the number for the school. The teacher was on his prep period and the office put Frank through to the class room.

"Kinnon," came the clipped answer on the third ring.

"Mr. Kinnon, this is Detective Frank Riley of the South Lake Tahoe Police Department. I wonder if you have a few minutes to answer some questions about one of your former students?"

"Be happy to help if I can," the man replied, "which student? I've had thousands through the years, and I am sorry to say, I don't remember them all."

"Do you remember Ken Lockwood?" asked Frank. It was worth a try.

"Yes, actually, I do." Mr. Kinnon said slowly. "He was a very troubled young man. Such a sad case."

"Can you expound on that please," asked Frank. The line was quiet for a few minutes.

"Well, I guess it would be okay, seeing as how you are a police officer and he is now a grown man." He paused again. "Ken was a very bright young man, but very troubled."

"How so?" asked Frank, listening carefully.

"His parents got into trouble with the law when Ken was in the eighth grade. They got arrested and sent to prison for drug dealing and manslaughter. By the time he got to high school and I met him, he had a lot of anger towards his parents for their illegal activities and breaking up the family."

"Was he ever violent?" asked Frank.

"No, almost the opposite," said Kinnon thoughtfully. "He was extremely intelligent, very quiet, a loner who pretty much stuck to himself and never got involved in school activities. He resented his parents for doing that to their family."

"Did Ken go to live with family after his parents went to prison?" asked Frank.

"No, poor kid had no other family," said the teacher, a note of sadness in his voice. "He was placed in a foster home."

"This is a curiosity question, but what subject do you teach?" asked Frank.

"Chemistry and biology," answered Mr. Kinnon. Frank's pencil froze above his note pad for a second, then he underlined the word chemistry.

"Did you ever work with the chemical compounds or formulas for chlorine or arsenic?" asked Frank.

Kinnon laughed. "Not really, detective, it was more basic chemistry, like what makes dry ice work, you know, everyday real life interactions." He cleared his throat. "My turn to ask a question," said Mr. Kinnon.

"Go ahead," said Frank. He knew what was coming.

"What is this all about, detective?" he asked.

"I'm investigating a murder," said Frank. "Ken knew the victim and I am just exploring all the options."

"You don't think Ken did it, do you?" asked Mr. Kinnon, with a tinge of alarm.

"I'm just checking the background and connections of all the people who knew the victim," hedged Frank.

"Would I know the victim, perhaps?" he asked.

"Maybe," replied Frank, "she also graduated from your high school. In fact, I wonder if you know if she and Ken knew each other in high school?"

"What was her name?" he asked.

"Ginger Snapper," Frank replied. The line was so quiet, Frank wondered if the connection had dropped. "Mr. Kinnon?"

"I'm here," came the breathless voice.

"Are you alright?

"Yes, but…,"he stopped. Frank waited. "Ginger and Ken did know each other in high school."

"Are you positive?" asked Frank, focusing intently.

"You know that foster home where they placed Ken?" The teacher was breathing loudly now. "Ginger Snapper's grandmother was the foster parent. They lived in the same house."

Chapter 28

Frank picked up his travel mug from his desk and walked into the break room. He picked up the coffee pot and looked at the thick, black burnt smelling sludge in the bottom of the carafe, and walked back out.

He kept walking all the way to the parking lot and got in his car. Driving gave him time to think, and he needed to work through motives for the murders. He and Jack had not gotten that far.

Now he knew Ken had known Ginger, but what did that mean? And how did that fit with Stephanie? Why hadn't Ken said anything about him and Ginger? But then, why would he?

Frank pulled into Alpina Coffee and parked. He walked up to the door with its hand carved cup of coffee that made him begin to salivate as he reached for the handle. He opened the door and was greeted with a delicious aroma of fresh coffee as he stepped into a coffee lovers paradise. Just the aroma of freshly ground coffee made him feel more relaxed. He stood just inside the door by the window counter and closed his eyes, then took a deep breath through his nose. He loved their Winter Blend, but it was months too soon for that tasty treat.

He sighed, opened his eyes, and walked up to the barista. He paid to fill the travel mug, then stepped down to the carafes sitting on the counter. He chose Sumatra and allowed himself an appreciative sip before he headed back outside. There was something about walking in and out of a coffee shop instead of going to a drive through; it was somehow more soothing. He needed this break with harsh reality once in awhile.

He drove over to We do it Your Way and saw Ken sitting on the front step, head in hand. He didn't even look up until Frank stood in front of him and waited.

"They can help you inside," Ken mumbled, still not looking up.

"I came to talk to you, Ken," said Frank. Ken still did not move for several more seconds. Then, he actually slumped and sighed before he sat up straight and looked up at Frank.

Ken's face was pale, his eyes were half shut, and he had dark circles under them. His elbows rested on his knees and his hands hung listlessly between his legs. He sighed again.

"How can I help you, detective?" he said with resignation.

"I'd like to ask you a few more questions," said Frank, studying him carefully. Frank was stunned at the apparent rapid deterioration of the young man.

"Of course," said Ken flatly. "Here or at the station?"

Frank glanced at the closed door and then back at Ken. "Are you working?"

"Working." Ken chuckled without mirth. "Not much. I am out here because they are in there arguing about how to replace me."

"Why would they do that?" asked Frank.

"They say they have complaints about my 'performance.' Apparently I'm not happy, animated, or peppy enough," replied the young man. He stared out at the street in front of them, but did not seem to register anything.

"I'd like to ask you why you didn't tell me you went to high school with Ginger Snapper," said Frank.

Ken's head jerked upward and he met Frank's eyes in surprise. He said nothing for a few minutes, then his shoulders sagged and he shook his head. He rubbed his eyes, and then stood decisively.

"Might as well be the station, then," he declared. "There's nothing good happening here and frankly, I don't want them to know all about my life." He walked resolutely towards Frank's car.

"Do you want to tell them you are leaving?" Frank called after him.

"Nah," answered Ken. "Who cares?" he said listlessly. Obviously, Ken did not.

Chapter 29

Ken sat in the chair beside Frank's desk and stared at the floor. Frank flipped the page on his legal pad to a fresh one and looked at Ken.

"Why didn't you tell me you knew Ginger Snapper in high school?" asked Frank.

"I hated high school. I didn't want anyone then to know I lived in a foster home, but they found out anyway," he answered. "When I graduated and turned eighteen, I moved away and started a new life, where no one knew anything about me."

"How did you come to work at the same agency as Ginger?"

"I have rotten luck," he said, waving his hands in the air. "I moved away, and found a job where nobody knew me."

"But Ginger worked there too, right?"

"Of course. She didn't know I worked there. One day I walked in and there she was. No one was around, so I asked her not to say she knew me."

"Wasn't it hard to keep that secret at work?" asked Frank.

"Not really. We didn't take the same kind of assignments; so no need to work together." He looked at Frank. "But then, her grandmother died and I just couldn't stay away."

"You went to her grandmother's funeral?" That was not something Frank expected to hear.

"Look, detective, I hated my parents for what they did to our family, to my life. I hated being in a foster home. I hated the cruel things the kids said and did to me because of all that." He bit his lip. "But, I am not a monster. Ginger's grandmother was the only person who ever really cared about me. I couldn't stay away. I needed to pay my last respects."

"You must have seen Ginger at the funeral," stated Frank.

"Of course I did. She wanted us to support each other, to be friends, because neither of us had anybody left."

"Did you spend more time together when you got back to town?"

"Just the opposite. I told her at the funeral that I wanted to forget my past, that I didn't want anyone in my life now to know anything about my life before." He shook his head. "I told her I didn't want to be friends, it was just too painful."

"Was she upset then?" asked Frank, studying Ken's haggard

face.

"No. She understood, and she honored my request."

"You never doubted her? You weren't afraid she would reveal your secret?"

Ken's face flushed with anger. "You think I killed Ginger to keep her quiet about my past?" He stared open mouthed at Frank. "Are you crazy?"

"It would be one way to keep your secret."

"She was always good to me!" Ken slammed his fist down on the desk and a few heads turned in the squad room. Frank held up a hand, palm out, and signaled all was under control. "I felt like such a heel when she was ... murdered."

"Did you have anything to do with it?" pushed Frank.

"No, detective, I did not! I don't know who killed that beautiful person or why. I just keep thinking if I had been friends, like she wanted, maybe I would have been there, and maybe..." He bent forward and hid his face in his hands. His body was shaking. "Don't you see?" he beseeched, looking up. "I could have just moved away again, or I could have been her friend and maybe this would not have happened." He looked at Frank with red rimmed eyes.

Frank waited and watched for several more minutes before he spoke. "Any idea who would hurt Ginger or Stephanie?" he asked.

"It doesn't make any sense. Ginger was sweet, kind, and honestly cared for people. She was just like her grandmother in that way." He sat quiet. "And Stephanie..." His voice trailed off and he just stared at a speck on the wall for several minutes. "She was beautiful, inside and out. I thought I finally found someone I could build a family with." He wiped tears off his face. "We were just beginning to get close. I asked her out and she said yes."

"When was that?" asked Frank.

"We were supposed to have our first date two days after she was poisoned."

He sat, defeated. Frank felt sorry for him. He also felt pretty sure he was not looking at a killer.

"What will you do now?" he asked Ken.

"I have no idea," said Ken. "Just figure out how to keep going on, I guess."

"Do you want a ride back to the office?"

"No," he answered. "I'm going to go home and take a few days to try to put my life back together. Alone."

"Can I give you a ride?" Frank felt like it was a small act of kindness. Ken seemed so hopeless right now.

"Sure," he shrugged, rising and plodding towards the door.

———————

Frank dropped Ken off in front of his apartment building and watched the young man move hypnotically up the steps and in the door.

He still had no motive for either of the crimes. Ken was right, his job wasn't worth killing someone over, he could have just moved on. Who would want two young women dead? Why?

He was lost in thought as he walked into the squad room again. He was only vaguely aware of passing the young woman sitting in the chair by the door. He sat down heavily at his desk and stared at his notepad.

"Detective Riley?" Frank looked up to see a pretty, young blond woman standing in front of his desk.

"Yes?" he said. "Is there something I can do for you?" He was bone weary.

"I think we need to talk," she said. He sighed, then stood and offered her a chair. She was very well dressed in a classic black suit with a crisp white blouse. Her two inch heels were fine leather and her overcoat was well tailored.

"What is this about?" Frank asked.

"I'm Justine Pullman," she said. Something clicked in Frank's memory.

"I just left you a message a few hours ago," he said. If he remembered correctly, she had an Iowa phone number.

"I didn't get it," she said, "I was already on my way here."

"Did you know Ginger then?" he asked. She nodded.

"Ginger Snapper was my best friend," she said. "And Nina Roberts is my mother."

Chapter 30

Frank simply stared at Justine for several long seconds. He was processing this unexpected news, attempting to fit it into the puzzle of facts he already knew. The young woman sat still, meeting his eyes with an openness that promised more to come.

"You are the daughter of Nina Roberts?" asked Frank. She certainly did not have her mother's temperament.

"Yes," repeated Justine, "and Ginger Snapper was my best friend."

"I didn't know Nina Roberts had a child," he speculated. "No children were listed when I did a background check," said Frank, beginning to have an odd feeling.

"She did not raise me," she said, continuing to hold his eyes, "I was raised in a foster home." She chewed on her lower lip as she switched her gaze to the window behind Frank. "That's how I met Ginger."

Frank's brain felt like it was shifting into high gear and racing down the track without his body. Pieces of the puzzle were falling into place faster than he could process and talk at the same time.

"Then you knew Ken Lockwood as well?" he asked.

"Of course," she nodded," he was a very unhappy boy who grew into a damaged adult, but yes, he was in the home with us."

"Was he ever violent, that you can recall?"

"Ken?" Her face held surprise, and her head moved back and forth. "No, not Ken," she said. "He was angry at his parents and his situation, but I think he really loved Ginger's grandmother." She was thoughtful as she unconsciously bit one of her nails. "No," she shook her head emphatically. I never saw Ken lose his temper and I never knew him to hurt any living thing." Her cool gray eyes locked on his. "Ken was the one that got hurt, by his parents, by life, and that made him 'damaged goods,' as they say."

"What do you mean by that?" asked Frank.

"He never felt accepted. He asked a girl out once and she jeered at him, said she would never go out with a 'foster boy; someone whose own parents didn't want him.' I had just come around the corner and saw and heard the whole thing. It was awful; his back was to me, and he didn't know I saw it happen. He never dated while we were in the home together."

"Never?"

"No, I don't think so. He was so incapable of trusting anyone."

*It must have been difficult, then, for him to actually ask
Stephanie out, he thought.* Frank was even more convinced that Ken was
not a killer. Frank's brain refocused.

"How old were you when you went to live in the foster home?"
asked Frank.

"I was six when I came to live in Mrs. Snapper's home," said
Justine. "I remembered my mother, but was glad to be away from her."
She looked down at her expensive shoes as if she was seeing them for
the first time. When she raised her eyes again, they were moist. "I also
remember that her boyfriend, my father, I guess, wasn't the only one
that hurt me."

"Are you saying your mother was abusive too?"asked Frank. He
never could understand what made a parent think it was okay to hurt
their own child. Actually, he didn't understand anyone who hurt
children.

Justine shifted uncomfortably in her chair. "They hit me, locked
me in dark closets, and I remember being really hungry many times."
She laughed with bitterness. "My 'mother' even scalded my arm once,
with water hot enough to hurt, but not leave a mark." Unconsciously,
she gently rubbed her left forearm through the sleeve of her suit coat.

"I'm sorry you had to go through that," said Frank with sincerity.
Justine nodded, but said nothing. "Did you ever see your mother again
after you were placed in the foster home?"queried Frank suddenly.

"Yes." Frank waited for her to be ready to continue. "One day
Ginger and I were in the kitchen with Mrs. Snapper, making a cake for a
birthday celebration for one of the kids in the home." She picked at
imaginary lint on her overcoat as she spoke. "There was a knock at the
door and Mrs. Snapper went to answer it. There was a loud voice but
Mrs. Snapper's voice was calm. I suppose we should have stayed in the
kitchen, but Ginger and I tiptoed out to the living room to see what was
going on."

"What happened?"

"There was a woman arguing with Mrs. Snapper. She said she
just wanted to see her daughter. Mrs. Snapper told her she needed to
leave." Justine gnawed on her lower lip so hard, Frank was afraid it

would start to bleed. "It was my fault," she said, looking down at her lap.

"I don't understand," said Frank, "did something happen? What was your fault?"

"Suddenly, I recognized her," she blew out a long breath. "I blurted it out, I yelled 'Mom!' I didn't know I had said it out loud until both of them stopped talking and looked at me." She shook her head. "Nina shoved past Mrs. Snapper and knelt in front of me, hugging me. She was blabbering about how she came to take me home. It was horrible. Mrs. Snapper was trying to separate us without hurting me, my mother would not let go, and I was crying." Frank offered Justine the box of tissues from his desk, and she wiped her eyes and nose.

"What happened next?" he coaxed.

"That's when things really got bad," she said, tears streaming down her face. "Mrs. Snapper called the police. I pulled away from my mother and Ginger and I were holding each other tight." She made a sound that was part whimper and part anguish. "Then I said it."

"What did you say?"

"I told my mother I didn't want to go live with her, I wanted to stay with Ginger, that she was my best friend."

Frank sat up straight. "How did Nina take that?"

"Her face turned real ugly, like it used to when she would hurt me." A choking sob escaped Justine's lips. "She grabbed my arm hard and I screamed. I don't know what she would have done if the police had not arrived at that point."

"The police arrested her?" asked Frank.

"I don't think so," replied Justine, I think they just made her leave."

"Did you ever see her again after that?" asked Frank, curious as to why she had not been arrested.

"No, "Justine stated," I had some nightmares for awhile after she came to the house." The sadness in her face tore at Frank's emotions. "I was afraid she would come back and take me away." Justine looked down at her hands in her lap and sat still for a few minutes. "Mrs. Snapper told me my mother was a long way away and that I was safe now. She finally told me she could not come back or the police would put her back in jail."

"Back in jail?" he studied the young woman. That could explain the sealed file. "Do you know why she was in jail?"

Justine shook her head. "No, Mrs. Snapper never told me why; she just said I shouldn't worry anymore, that no one could take me away."

"Did you ever see your father after you were taken away to the foster home?"

"I guess I never really thought about it, but no," she said, confusion on her face. They sat in silence for a few minutes, both lost in their thoughts. A piece fell in place.

"Ginger and Ken both worked for your mother, then. Did she make the connection to the foster home?"

Justine sighed and picked at her immaculate fingernails. "With Ken, no, I am certain of that. She never saw him at the home and he has kept his personal background a secret. Ginger told me that. She said she saw him at the agency, but he didn't see her. Something told her not to say anything, you know, sometimes you just get a feeling." She shrugged her shoulders and studied the wall for a moment. "Then, at the funeral for Mrs. Snapper, he begged her not to tell anyone they knew each other or how they grew up. He didn't want anyone to know they grew up in the same home."

"What about Ginger?" asked Frank, holding his breath a little.

"That's the thing," said Justine, "when Ginger told me where she was working, I told her that was crazy and to find another job." Justine wiped away another tear. "Ginger came to visit my husband and me after we had our baby. We talked at length about this, and she promised she would get another job soon."

"Did Nina recognize Ginger?" asked Frank.

"Ginger didn't think so, but I…," she whimpered again. "I told Ginger I thought she must remember her and that I was afraid for her."

"Why were you afraid for Ginger?" asked Frank.

"Because, detective, the night I told my mother I wanted to stay with my friend," she was sobbing now, the words coming out in gulps. "We were only eight years old!" she hiccupped. "Just as the police grabbed my mother to take her away, she leaned down to Ginger and she said…" she was wiping tears away with both hands. "My mother hissed at Ginger. I don't think anyone else heard her and we never told anyone."

"What did Nina say to Ginger?"

"She said, 'I'll kill you, you little bitch, for keeping my daughter away from me!'"

"*S*he said that to Ginger?" Frank gasped. "She was a child!" Justine shrugged and put her hands up in a helpless gesture.

"I know, but Ginger just wouldn't believe she would remember her because she thought she looked so different grown up. I tried to tell her how vicious my mother could be."

"Didn't Ginger remember what Nina had said to her?" Frank had a cold feeling about this.

" Neither of us ever forgot what she said. I asked Ginger when she came to visit if she remembered, and she got a faraway look in her eye and nodded her head. Then she tried to laugh it off, but I could tell it still bothered her."

Frank considered this for several minutes. "Do you have any idea at all why Nina was ever in jail?" That unknown detail nagged at him.

"No, I really couldn't say," answered Justine, "but nothing would surprise me." She shivered. "I know she is my mother and all, but that woman is inherently evil."

An idea was forming in the back of Frank's mind, but he could not act on the hunch immediately. "Does your mother know you are here?" he asked.

"No, we have never tried to make contact with her. I don't even think she knows I have a child, and I want to keep it that way." She looked at Frank.

"She won't hear it from me," he said, answering the unspoken question. "Do you know her husband, Chad?" he pursued, exploring all options while he had her in front of him.

"No, I never met him. Ginger talked about him, though. I think that is one of the reasons she stayed at the agency as long as she did. Chad made her feel a little safer."

"Did she ever tell you about the incident where Chad took her to a motel?"

"Yes, my mother was in rare form that day!" Justine sputtered, a flash of anger in her eyes. "She cornered Ginger and was shouting at her, calling her names. According to Ginger, my mother is apparently jealous of all the women; she thinks they are all after Chad, or he is after them," she said with disgust.

"So Nina was jealous of Ginger?"

"Yes, which was so stupid. Ginger wasn't like that. When she talked about Chad, it was to say what a truly nice guy he is, and he was never inappropriate with any of the girls at the agency." She was silent for a moment, then shook her head decisively. "No, she said Chad was more like a big brother to the girls. Protective."

"Did she ever mention Nina going after any of the other girls?" he asked.

"Come to think of it, no!" Her eyes widened at the thought. "Do you think she really did know it was my Ginger, my friend?"

"I think I have some more work to do," he said thoughtfully. "How long are you going to be in town?"

"Well, that depends," she said sadly. "Ginger had no one else. My husband and I would like to make her final arrangements, but we don't know what paperwork we need to file. Can you help us?" She opened her mouth to say something, stopped, then decided to speak. "Can you keep this confidential, detective? I really don't want anyone to know we are here."

"Yes," Frank said and picked up the phone on his desk. "Bruce, I'm on my way over with a couple who would like to claim the remains of Ginger Snapper." Justine winced as he spoke, knotting her hands together. He hung up and stood. "Please come with me."

Chapter 31

Frank and Justine walked out to the reception area, where a tall, lean, young man sat protectively holding a bundle of blankets. He got to his feet as they came through the door, concern on his tanned face as his eyes searched Justine's countenance.

"Detective Riley, this is my husband, Rory Pullman," she said as she reached for the bundle. Rory relinquished it to Justine, but kept his eyes on her face.

"I'm okay," she smiled to her husband. She patted the blankets as Rory turned to Frank.

"It's a pleasure to meet you, Sir," said Rory, as he stuck out his hand. "My wife needed to tell you her story."

"She has been very helpful," said Frank, "the case is coming together much better now." He glanced at the bundle, which was now beginning to squirm.

"This is our son, Marcus," she said, smiling at the little face peeking out from the blankets. "Detective Riley has promised to keep our visit confidential." Frank held up both hands, palms out, and shook his head in agreement. He saw relief flood over Rory's countenance as the young man smiled at Justine.

"I would have no reason whatsoever to tell your mother about your son, nor for that matter, that any of you are even here." He looked from one to the other. "I don't blame you one bit for not wanting Nina in your lives."

Both Justine and Rory visibly relaxed, and Rory put his arm around Justine's shoulders. Frank observed the unspoken communication between them. They stood, their eyes moving, but only for each other, until Justine nodded, very subtly. Rory responded with a decisive dipping of his head, and then, his arm still around Justine's shoulders, he turned to Frank.

"Detective Riley, would you be so kind as to point us in the direction of the facility that has Ginger's remains?" Rory's formality seemed an effort to somehow sterilize the situation. Frank appreciated the attempt to put himself between the sad circumstances and his wife's grief.

"I can do better than that; I'll walk you over to the Medical Examiner's building," said Frank. "Are you ready?"

Another look passed between the couple, and then they nodded in unison. "Yes," said Rory and Justine in sync. Rory reached for Marcus again, and held the infant with one arm, while he placed his other hand in the small of his wife's back for support and comfort.

Frank envied them their amazing non verbal communication. He went through first and held the door for them, as they came out on the sidewalk.

"Do you think this will be a problem?" asked Justine anxiously. "I mean, we aren't family, exactly." She searched his face.

"The Medical Examiner and the Department of Social Services prefers to have family or friends tend to the final arrangements. I don't think there will be a problem." Noting the concern remaining on her face, he continued. "This happens more often than you would think. We have released remains to friends before; we are very grateful when someone who cares can take the person home." He held her gaze until he saw understanding spread across her face. Not everyone had someone who loved them like she loved Ginger. "It won't be an issue," he said softly. The steps to the ME building were taken in silence.

Frank opened the door and allowed the couple to pass through first this time. He stepped in behind them and stopped in his tracks. Sierra was standing in the foyer, hands resting in each other at waist level, and wearing a subdued smile. The stark change in her since he had seen her two days ago was stunning. Dark circles sat beneath her eyes in a pale, drawn, face. Her eyes met his briefly, and left him more concerned at the vacant, guarded depths.

"I'm Doctor O'Malley," she said with reserve, extending a slim, white hand to the Pullmans. "I know this will be difficult for you," she said, directing her comment to Justine, "But I am so glad that Ms. Snapper has someone to care for her. Please follow me."

Justine and Rory exchanged a look and Frank noted a deep sigh escape from Justine, as they began the slow walk down the hall. The identification took only a few minutes, and they were soon seated at Sierra's desk, with paperwork spread in front of them. It was surprisingly easy for them to complete the paperwork and claim the body. The reality was, the state was generally happy to have someone claim an unattended body and save them the expense of a burial or cremation. He listened as Justine and Rory asked questions and then signed the papers to have Ginger's body cremated.

"We couldn't stand the thought of leaving her in a lonely grave," explained Justine. "We are going to put her in a nice urn so she can always be with us." Rory patted her back as she spoke, and they nodded at each other.

Frank cleared the knot in his throat as they all stood. The Pullman's shook hands with Sierra and Frank, then started for the door.

"Thank you again," she said, switching her eyes from Frank to Sierra and back again. Her eyes held Frank's as her face became set. "Detective Riley?"

"Yes? Is there something else I can do for you?" he answered. He respected this young couple, and wanted to help in any way he was able.

Justine nodded, and her eyes glistened with anger. "Get the person who did this." For the second time, Frank was given a task he truly hoped he could accomplish.

He watched them walk towards the parking lot for a few minutes, then turned towards the desk. Sierra had vanished. He felt uneasy, and fought a desire to find her. He lost the battle with himself, and headed down the hall to find the ME. She could very well tell him to go to hell, but he knew there was something wrong and he had to offer his help again.

Frank was passing the elevator when the doors opened and he turned. Bruce stepped through the doors and smiled as he saw Frank.

"Hi Frank," he said, "did you get the matter wrapped up regarding Ginger Snapper?"

"Yes," he hesitated. "Bruce, I couldn't help but notice how ragged Sierra looks. I am really worried."

"I am too," replied the younger man, glancing down the hall. "I caught her crying in her office yesterday. It was after quitting time and I think she thought there was no one here. I had stayed a little over to finish a test and I wanted her to see the results first thing in the morning. I thought she was gone for the day, so I opened the door without knocking." He blew out a breath and searched Frank's eyes. "She had her arms crossed on her desk, with her head down. She was sobbing, Frank. I haven't heard a woman cry like that since my wife's cousin lost her baby to SIDS."

"What did she do when you opened the door?"

"She jumped! Our eyes locked for a second, then she quickly spun her chair around and pretended to be looking for something on the shelf behind her desk. I asked her if she was okay, and she almost shouted that she was fine! Then she barked at me that I shouldn't be there, she wasn't going to authorize the overtime. She never turned back to look at me."

"Did you notice anything else?"Frank prodded.

Bruce stood thinking for a few moments, then slowly began to nod his head. "Yeah," he said tentatively, then more assertively repeated himself. "Yeah, I am sure there was a snapshot, like a school picture, of a young boy, clutched in her hand. Her hand was outstretched a little when I walked in. She slipped it in her pocket fast, as she turned the chair towards the wall."

"Sounds like something to do with a child in her life then," Frank mused out loud.

"I told her I brought her the test results and lay them on her desk. She did not turn around, so I asked her if she was alright, and if I could help." Bruce began to walk towards his desk and Frank stepped beside him.

"What did she say?"

" She told me to go home, that we had a busy morning the next day." He looked at Frank. "I'm worried about her."

"Thanks Bruce," said Frank, staring at the ceiling for a minute. "This helps me know my instincts are right on."

"Frank…," Bruce hesitated. "There's something else." He looked at the floor, chewed on his lip for a minute, then stared at the detective. "Her sleeve was pushed up a bit and she had her lab coat off. I could swear there were bruises on her wrist." He shook his head. "Can you help her, Frank?" asked the young assistant.

"I'm going to try," Frank promised.

"What are you going to do?" asked Bruce hopefully.

Frank glanced at him. "Probably get myself in a lot of trouble," he answered grimly, as he headed for the door. It was better that Bruce did not know.

Chapter 32

Frank sat in the darkness, watching the house. He had gone home, showered, eaten, changed, and slept for three hours before he filled a thermos with coffee and set out on his mission.

He poured a little more coffee in the small cup from the top of the thermos. He wondered if a cop had invented the idea of the cup on top of the thermos, since almost every undercover cop he knew carried one on stake out. The size of the cup kept the coffee hot and kept them from drinking too much at once, then needing to find a bathroom. It was one of the problems with being in a car, just watching, for long periods of time.

The lights had been off in the house for several hours now and the chill of the night crept into the car. He zipped his windbreaker to just below his throat, but he did not start the car to turn on his heater. Anyone who noticed his car, would have to be very close to see him slumped below the head rest in the driver's seat, but a running car would be a dead giveaway.

He was taking a big chance, and he knew it, but he just couldn't walk away. If his Captain ever found out he had used the department resources to find the home address for Sierra O'Malley, he could kiss his detective shield goodbye for a good long while, if not forever.

His mind drew up details of every encounter with the ME. He analyzed her face, her expressions, and came to the conclusion that she had changed drastically from the first day he met her. The fire in her green eyes had faded in the short time since they met in Ginger's apartment. It was not the stress of the job, he was sure of that. She had been a Medical Examiner for several years, according to her personnel file. The murders, while not simple, were also not grisly. Her demeanor as she worked with the cadavers was matter of fact; professional and appropriately detached.

And, he admitted to himself, *you find her attractive.* Physically, she was pretty, no doubt about that. Her dark, soft waves of hair set off those green eyes in a way that was captivating. She was a rare combination of physical attraction, compassion, and intellect. *Damn it.*

Yet, her peaches and cream healthy complexion had disappeared and her cheeks were now pale and concave. There were dark circles under her eyes, and although he had never seen her in anything that actually revealed her slender figure, he was positive she had lost weight. He would not be able to explain the gut feeling to a lay person, but his cop senses told him it was not illness, but something emotional or mental that brought about the change in her in a few short weeks.

He studied the simple, one story wood home where the ME lived. It was painted beige with dark green trim, and had a few pine trees to one side of the house. The front yard was neat and held a few flower beds with rock for accent. There were bushes of tall Lupine close to the house in front of the windows. *Her car must be in the attached garage. That was a good move; garages were a rare commodity in Tahoe.*

Sudden movement low on the ground near the bushes under a front window caught his attention. He squinted to make out the slow moving form slinking along the side of the house. He debated a minute about opening the door. If he did and she looked through the window or came outside, it would mean at least a suspension for him if she complained. He hesitated, then reached up and turned out the overhead light in the car. He grasped the handle, his eyes glued to the skulking shadow, and silently opened the car door, staying curled around the form of the door so his silhouette would not be seen.

He carefully stepped out beside the car and gently closed the door, then, still crouching, he ran through the yard his car was parked in front of and vaulted a small fence. He stopped behind a picket fence with rose bushes and peered through the prickly branches. Was that a man, half crawling beside the house? The bulky figure stood on two legs, but still slightly bent, right beside a window and appeared to be tampering with the screen.

Frank rose, and took a step forward, drawing his gun at the same time. He was instantly blinded by floodlights that flashed on all around the house. He put his hand up to shield his eyes and crouched again as the figure dropped down and ran from the house. He nearly burst out laughing as he watched the bear run down the street.

His laughter was short lived; the curtain in the living room moved slightly and he was certain Sierra or someone else in the house was peering out into the street. *She must have some kind of interior alarm system that was triggered by the scratching at the screen. Good move, Sierra.* He holstered his gun and stayed behind the rose bush, waiting for her to turn out the flood lights and go back to bed.

He wasn't going to be that lucky. He shifted slightly, and then froze. The low growl coming from behind him was not friendly.

Moisture formed on his forehead. What kind of dog was behind him? Where was its owner? He twisted slowly, rising carefully to his full height. The growling got louder.

"Good boy," he cajoled, "It's okay, I'm a cop," he cooed. The Australian Healer was not impressed and snapped, then started barking as he inched closer to Frank's leg. "Oh, this is just great." He could hear sirens coming closer. He tried to take a step backward and the dog leapt forward, sinking his teeth into Frank's leg. Even through his thick jeans, he could feel the teeth pierce the skin of his calf.

"Freeze, Mister!" Again, Frank had a bright light in his face as a porch light went on in the house that was behind the yard. "You take one more step and I'll tell Molly there to tear off your foot!" Frank looked in disbelief at the aged man in rumpled pajamas, holding a shotgun leveled at him. "That is, if I don't shoot you myself," he grinned.

"I'm a cop," said Frank, "just call off your dog and I'll show you my badge."

"Do you think I just fell off the pumpkin truck?" the man sneered at him. "You probably have a gun hidden and if Molly backs off, you'll try to shoot me!"

Two squad cars screamed up the street, one stopping in front of Sierra's house and the other skidding to a halt in front of the neighbor's house. An officer sprang from the driver's seat, and semi crouched behind the open door of the squad car.

"Drop the gun, now!" the officer barked at the old man, aiming a pistol in the man's direction, but staying behind and to the left of Frank.

The old man bent and placed the shotgun on the ground, then raised his hands in the air.

"Now we'll just see who the real cops are!" He pointed at Frank. "That man was in the bushes there, sneaking around my house!" he yelled.

"I'm a police officer," Frank said wincing in pain, "I'm going to reach under my shirt so you can see my badge." The young officer was peering at him through the dark.

"Detective Riley?"

"Yes!" Frank still could not see his face in the dim light, but the voice was vaguely familiar. "Could you help me out here?" he said, pointing to the dog that was still pulling on his pant leg. The dog had released his teeth to get a better grip, apparently, and now just had the cloth in his mouth, pulling and wrestling like Frank's pant leg was a chew toy.

"It's Officer Rayburn, Sir." He turned to the old man watching from the porch. "Sir, please call off your dog!"

"Sure thing, officer. Molly!" he commanded, "Come!" he patted his leg and Molly released the jeans, looking from her master to Frank, then turned and trotted back to sit by the man on the porch.

"Thanks, Rayburn," said Frank, bending to look at his leg. Blood was running down his calf and into his sock. "Sir," he said to the man on the porch, "I'm going to need to see the rabies records for your dog."

"Oh. Of course! Let me get them," said the man, disappearing into the house and taking Molly with him.

"Here comes Smitty with the owner of the home across the street," said Rayburn, holstering his weapon.

"M'am, is this the man you have a restraining order against?" asked Smitty.

Frank saw Rayburn shoot him a puzzled look. He cringed when he heard her voice, and his stomach felt like it was twisting in knots.

"I don't believe it!" Sierra moved in front of him. "It IS you! Frank Riley, of all the dirty tricks! Do you think it's funny to sneak around my house and scare me to death?"

"No, I swear, it was a bear that triggered your alarm!" pleaded Frank.

"And how would you know that, Detective?" Sierra stood with her arms crossed over her chest, a dark green bathrobe belted around her body against the cold. Her eyes glittered at him and her lips stretched to a thin line across her face, crimson with anger.

"What's going on here, Detective Riley?" asked Rayburn, glancing at Smitty. "Why are you here, Sir?" His voice had taken on an official tone.

Frank stood, looking at her face, then at the two officers. He was in deep here, and he knew it. He had to choose his words carefully.

Frank faced the three of them, as they all stood staring at him with accusation on their faces. To make it worse, the old man chose that moment to return with a sheet of paper in his hand. He stopped as he felt the tension, and shifted his gaze back and forth between the two groups. He quickly read the situation and sided with Sierra and the other two officers. He folded his arms across his chest and glared at Frank triumphantly.

"Sierra," Frank began, "Bruce and I are both worried about you."

His attempt to break the tension was not successful.

"So, your idea is to come and set off my alarm and scare me half to death?" Her hands were now on her hips, her body rigid with anger.

"No, I just wanted to make sure you were safe!" he protested.

"How did you know where I live?" she accused. Rayburn and Smitty exchanged a look, and Smitty stepped off to one side, walking several steps away from the group. Frank knew what he was doing, even though he could not hear what he was saying into his shoulder mic.

"That isn't important," he bluffed, "I had to know you were safe." It was lame and he knew it. Rayburn and Smitty fixed him with withering gazes and tight lips. Sierra was livid, clenching her hands into fists. Smitty spoke first.

"Detective Riley, you may go tonight, but we have orders to convey that you are to be in the Chief's office at eight o'clock tomorrow morning." He turned to Sierra. "Is that satisfactory to you, M'am?"

Sierra glared for several full seconds at Frank before she answered the officer. "Of course. Thank you officers, for your very professional conduct." It was a polite gesture to the officers, but a pointed dig at Frank. She turned and walked back to her home, slamming the door as she stepped inside.

The neighbor handed the rabies verification to Rayburn and smirked at Frank as he turned back to his warm home as well. Rayburn glanced at the paper, then extended it to Frank.
The two officers stood, waiting and watching him. Frank colored as he realized they were waiting for him to leave the scene.

"Thank you," he spoke through gritted teeth, accepting the paper. Humiliated, he walked to his car, started the engine, and hurriedly drove away.

He steered the car towards Barton Hospital. Even though it wasn't really an emergency, he knew the dog bite needed to be examined. In his line of work, it wasn't the first time a dog had bitten him, and the common course was to dress the wound and prescribe antibiotics.

"At least I have never had to get rabies shots," he grumbled. It was going to be a long night, but he knew he would not sleep well anyway. He had been commanded to meet with the Chief, not just his Captain. This was going to be bad.

Chapter 33

Frank showed up ten minutes early for the meeting next morning, limping slightly. The ER doctor had cleaned the wound and decided he needed four stitches. In spite of the antibiotics, the bite area felt like it was on fire and was red and angry looking this morning.

He was dressed in his best suit and freshly shaven, hoping the show of respect would get him a point or two. Those hopes fell as he looked through the window and saw his Captain and Sierra already seated in the office, with the Chief behind his desk. Their collective body language told him he was about to get his ass handed to him. He knocked softly, and entered at a nod from the Chief.

"Have a seat, Frank," said the Chief, gesturing towards the lone remaining chair, set at an angle that faced the three occupants of the room. The Chief was a solidly built man in his mid-fifties, with salt and pepper hair. His face was lined with years of hard work and his piercing gray eyes were accentuated by the thick black eyebrows that sat above them. Frank read nothing in the Chief's face or his steady gaze, nor did his Captain or Sierra give him any clue in their expressions. It was the way they held themselves, still and rigid, and all three had their arms crossed over their chests; Sierra drumming her fingers on her arms. He took a deep breath and lowered himself into the chair, feeling like he had just been kicked in the stomach.

"Do you understand why you are here, Frank?" The question came from his Captain. There was no give in his expression. None of Frank's expertise at reading people was helping him now.

"Yes, Sir," Frank replied, careful to keep an even tone.

"Did you use the police department computer to access the personnel files of Doctor Sierra O'Malley?"

"Yes, I did." He kept his eyes away from her as he replied to the questions.

"Is that how you got her address?" the Captain's gaze was level and cold.

"Yes, Sir." He knew it would only make it worse to attempt to cover up what he had done.

"Did you go to her home of your own accord?" The Captain glanced at Sierra, then turned his eyes back to Frank. "On your own time?"

"That is correct, Captain." The acid from his coffee that morning felt like it was burning a hole through his stomach.

"Do you have anything to say for yourself?" asked the Chief. Frank turned his head and studied the Chief's stony expression for a few moments, then rested his eyes first on his Captain, then Sierra. She looked fragile; her skin sallow and her thick, dark hair seemed lifeless, lacking its usual sheen and bounce. Her eyes were flat, and she looked, to him, sleep deprived and thinner than she had been two weeks ago. He held her gaze several seconds before he spoke.

"Yes, Sir, I do." The silence was thick as he looked at each face. He felt his temper rising and fought to keep it under control as he spoke. "I am a cop. No, I am a detective, and a damn good one at that."

Uncertainty registered on the Captain's face, while the Chief remained unreadable. Sierra stopped drumming her fingers on her arms and seemed to freeze as she watched him.

"I noticed peculiar behavior in one of our employees," Frank continued, "I saw her one night, quite by accident, I will add, walking from the building with body language that said she was disturbed. Yet, when I broached the subject at what I thought was an opportune time, she basically told me it was none of my business."

"Why didn't you leave it at that?" interjected the Captain.

"I did. At least until both her assistant and I noticed a marked change in her physical appearance." He looked directly at Sierra now, who seemed to be holding her breath. All color had gone from her face. "Look at her, and tell me her physical appearance is not one that raises flags in your cop gut." Sierra's lips parted and her tongue ran nervously over dry lips. "She has become pale, subdued, and unless I miss my guess, she has lost weight in the past two weeks."

Both officers turned, did a quick visual inspection of her, and exchanged looks between themselves before turning back to Frank. "Her assistant told me he walked in her office after hours a few nights ago and found her crying at her desk," Frank continued. He looked directly at her. "Ms. O'Malley," he said very softly, "do you have bruises on your wrist?"

A small cry escaped her lips as Sierra brought a hand to her mouth. The motion caused the cuff of the blouse she was wearing to slide down her arm a few inches, revealing a purplish yellow bruise. No one moved.

"I ask you, gentlemen, if this was anyone other than an

employee, would you not have expected me to pursue the safety of what has every appearance of being an abused woman?"

Chapter 34

The silence was suffocating as all three officers turned their eyes on Sierra. But her eyes were only on Frank, and the accusation and pain in them was killing him. When she started to shake and tears slid down her cheeks, it took everything he had to keep from gathering her in his arms and telling her it would be okay.

"Ms. O'Malley," said the Chief gently, breaking his silence. Both Sierra and Frank turned their heads in his direction, and Frank was surprised at the kindness in the man's eyes. "Are you alright? Would you like a glass of water?" he continued softly, as if he was afraid she would break if he spoke too loud. She nodded her head, and Frank jumped to his feet, only too glad to do something useful, and eager to get out of the room for a few minutes.

He stepped out of the door and walked quickly to the water cooler, filling the paper cup, and carrying it swiftly back to the small room. He held it in front of her, and she accepted it without looking at him. Self consciously, she drank most of the water before she set the cup on the file cabinet next to her. It was obvious she was frightened; her hands were shaking so badly Frank thought the water would slosh over the top of the cup. She sniffed and let out a ragged sigh and the Captain hurriedly took the box of tissues off the Chief's desk and held it out to her. His reward was a weak smile.

The men waited patiently, knowing she would speak when she was ready. Sierra dabbed at her eyes and nose, and shook her head, then finally brought her gaze up to Frank. He saw the raw pain now, and he swallowed hard, as if he had a glob of peanut butter stuck in his throat.

"I wish you weren't always so damned good at your job," she chided Frank, but then gave him a wry smile. "Detective Riley has good instincts," she said, looking at the Chief and the Captain, "unfortunately for me." Frank shifted uncomfortably in his chair while Sierra twisted the tissue in her hand. She seemed to come to a decision suddenly, setting her lips in a hard line.

"I am being stalked," she said simply. All three men sat up straighter in their chairs and gave her their full attention. "Six years ago, my fiancé was killed in a car accident. Shortly after, I found out I was pregnant." She held her head up and looked at them with a fierceness that made Frank almost want to smile. "I took two years off school to have my son, and was planning to start back to finish my education. Then, a brother I did not even know my fiancé had, showed up at my home one day, demanding to see his brother's son. It was a total shock; I did not know the man existed, and he was demanding I turn my son over to him." She caught her breath and looked down at her lap for several moments, wiping at her eyes again.

Frank looked from the Chief to the Captain, gauging their reaction. The Chief dipped his head in Frank's direction and his Captain nodded at him. Feeling united in concern for her safety, Frank again turned his eyes on Sierra.

"My neighbor was there, fixing a faucet for me, while his wife and I chatted over coffee.   George, the brother, caught sight of my son, who had come to the door behind me when he heard our voices. It was awful." She stopped and stared at a spot on the wall while she seemed to think about what to say next. She took a deep breath and let it out slowly.

"Take your time," said the Chief, trying his best to sound soothing and empathetic. Sierra nodded, then waited several long seconds before she continued.

"George started screaming at me, he said I was a …a slut that was trying to trick his brother into marrying me. He said I was just after the family money!" She looked around the room, settling on Frank. "I didn't even know Geoffrey had a brother, much less any money!" She shook her head. "It would not have made a difference to me; we were in love." Her shoulders shook as she sobbed softly. Several minutes passed as they gave her time to regroup. She brought her sobbing under control, and let out a sigh that sounded much like a whimper, raising her head to look at them.

"Is he the one stalking you?" asked Frank quietly.

"Yes," she said. "I'm sure of it now." She sat immobile, immersed in her own thoughts, as if she were alone.

"What else can you tell us?" prompted the Captain, as minutes went by and she did not offer any other information.

"He wanted my son," she said mournfully. "George was yelling at me, saying that Garrett is the only heir that will carry on the family line, and he should be raised with all the advantages George could give him."

"Did you call the police?" asked Frank.

"No," said Sierra, shaking her head. My neighbor came to the door and told George to leave. Harry is a pretty big guy," she smiled. "George left, but he was screaming that he would get Garrett if it is the last thing he did."

"Is that why you left Cambridge?" asked Frank. As soon as the words left his mouth, Sierra's eyebrows shot up. Frank mentally kicked himself, afraid to look at his Captain.

"How did you…?" she stopped, her mouth open as she starred at him.

"Riley, what the hell…" began the Captain, anger flushing his face.

"No…no," Sierra said, holding one hand up in the direction of the Captain, as she gave him a look of contrition. "I remember now; Frank and I were talking one day about where I got my degree." She lied smoothly as she held Frank's eyes. He didn't know why she had just lied for him, but he was so grateful at that moment, he would have kissed her feet if she asked.

"I'm sorry for the interruption," the Captain said, still glowering at Frank, suspicion clearly hovering in his mind.

"To answer the question," she said, "yes, that is why I left Cambridge. I thought coming clear across the United States would make it difficult for George to find us."

"Did you come straight to Tahoe?" asked Frank, knowing the answer, but wanting to appear like he did not. He was on thin ice, and he didn't dare give away any other details he had found while doing his computer search.

"No," she answered, a flicker of amusement in her eyes. "I finished my doctorate at Stanford."

"Were there any incidents with this George character while you were there?" the Chief inquired.

"No, but…" she hesitated. "I went through the Women's Center and they changed my name and all my records. I took my mother's maiden name, which I didn't think George would know."

"Your name isn't really Sierra O'Malley?" asked Frank in surprise. *They did a good job on those records!*

"No. I was born Sierra Brogan. My father actually suggested the name change when I told my parents what was going on."

"Smart," murmured Frank, "but what about your son? Couldn't George find him with his father's last name? Or, didn't you…" He let the question hang, feeling a little foolish at the assumption she would give the boy his father's name.

"It's funny," she smiled, "I did give Garret his father's last name on his birth certificate, but when we moved to Palo Alto, he had not yet started school. An attorney through the Women's Center helped us get an altered birth certificate created with my new last name. It's temporary, but the attorney convinced the judge it was just to protect us, not for any real legal documentation."

"Will that be a problem when you tell your son about all this someday?" Frank blurted the question impulsively, and received a withering look from his Captain. *Just shut up, Frank! Are you trying to sound like an idiot who wants to lose his shield?*

"I don't think so. He can go by my name until he is sixteen and goes to get a driver's license. I have kept his original birth certificate, and when I am sure he is safe, I will tell him about his father."

"I'm a little confused," said the Captain, "if he didn't show up in Palo Alto, why do you think he is here? Have you seen him?"

"Yes." A shudder shook her as she dipped her head for a moment. "First it was just the silent phone calls. But then, four days ago he surprised me getting into my car after work." Her voice broke and she raised a hand to her lips as if to make her mouth calm. "He grabbed my wrist and was shaking me."

"If you had screamed, cops would have come running," said Frank, a puzzled look on his face.

"I didn't want anyone to know," she said in a small voice.

She's ashamed! The realization struck him like a bucket of ice water in the face. He stared at her as she dropped her head and twisted the tissue again. He met the eyes of his fellow officers, and saw they all shared an obvious sadness.

"What happened next?" Frank prodded gently.

"A police car pulled into the lot and he ran away," she stammered.

"Did they see him?" he pried carefully, trying not to push her too hard.

"No. But he ran away and I got in my car and drove away. I was afraid to go home until I was sure I wasn't being followed."

A thought struck him "When did you have the alarm system put in?" he asked.

"I left work early a couple of days ago and had it done," she answered. "Just in time for you to set it off." She looked at him with raised eyebrows and a glimmer of a smile playing across her lips.

"Hey, it really was a bear!" he protested. "I thought someone was crawling in the bushes in front of your house, but I couldn't quite make out the shape as it stood on its hind legs and picked at your screen. When the lights went on, it ran away, and I could see it was a bear, but by then…" He stopped as he realized all of them were staring at him with total deadpan expressions. He ran his hand over his face, pinching the bridge of his nose before he dared look back at his Captain.

"Well," said the Chief, clearing his throat and glaring at Frank, "Ms. O'Malley, forgive me," he said, bringing his gaze back to her, "but it sounds as if you need some protection," he said softly. His eyes were pleading with her to give them permission to help. "Can you give me George's last name please?"

"It's Morgan. George Morgan."

"Do you know his approximate age?"

"Yes, he is thirty-seven."

"How can you be sure of that?" asked the Captain.

She looked at the Captain, then reached down to pick up her purse. She retrieved her wallet and opened it, where she stared at what appeared to be a picture, before removing it from its plastic sleeve, and extending it to the Chief. He took the picture, then gave her a puzzled look.

"George is Geoffrey's identical twin brother; that is how I know his age. I nearly fainted when I opened the door." She caught her breath, then sighed before going on. "That picture is of me with Geoffrey. George looks just like his brother."

The Chief wrote something down, then hit a button on his desk. Within moments, a young officer in uniform entered the room. Without saying a word, the Chief handed the note to the officer and the young woman left the room, without making eye contact with anyone.

"Ms. O'Malley, I'd like to assign someone to protection duty until we catch this guy," said the Chief. He glared at Frank. "I mean, officially." The inference was not lost on Frank, who shrunk down in his seat a little.

"Thank you, but I'll be fine, Chief…" she began.

"Ms. O'Malley," the Chief interrupted her. His tone carried a slightly stern quality now. "No one in this room believes that, including you." His gray eyes bore into her. "We protect our own."

She nodded in resignation, twisting the tissue again. Silence took over the room again, with a strange heaviness.

"Can I go now?" she finally asked, in a subdued voice.

The Chief tapped a pen on his desk and looked at the Captain, who shrugged his shoulders. "Are you satisfied with the action taken here today?" he asked. She shot Frank a quick look, then nodded at the Chief.

"I think Detective Riley had my best interests in mind, even though his methods were a bit unusual," she offered.

"To say the least," muttered the Captain under his breath. Frank heard the comment and a thin sheen of moisture coated his forehead.

"Then thank you, Ms. O'Malley, said the Chief, standing. Frank and the Captain leapt to their feet as Sierra rose slowly. "I will have someone get in touch with you before the end of the day so you know who is on your side."

"Thank you," she said, "I should go; Bruce will be wondering where I am." Frank held the door for her as she left quietly, head drooping a bit. He shot an inquiring look at his superiors. Without a word, the Chief pointed at the chair he had recently vacated. Frank felt the acid rise in his throat as he took the seat again, and faced the two men who could destroy his career.

Chapter 35

Frank was only too glad to have a reason to step outside and breathe some fresh air. Even though Sierra had covered for him and been content with the process, the Captain and Chief had spent a very painful fifteen minutes chewing him up and spitting him out. He was informed that this would never be overlooked again, and he was to consider himself damn lucky he was only getting a verbal warning, instead of an official written reprimand in his file.

The saving grace was that his superiors truly believed Sierra was in danger, and that gave him a very small leeway. Along with his stellar record, they grudging let the incident become a verbal warning only, instead of the write up and suspension he deserved.

He knew he was lucky; this could have been a career ending fiasco. He had been stupid to go about it the way he had. He should have involved his Captain, but he had let his personal feelings get in the way. He had to step back and let his Captain arrange for protection for Sierra. *You do have a case to close,* he reminded himself.

He made a phone call and then got behind the wheel, easing out of the parking lot. He wound his way through the streets towards Jack's house, in no hurry. He was giving himself time to shift gears from the incident surrounding Sierra, back to his primary focus, the murder case he needed to solve. Sometimes, if he just let his mind wander and look at the scenery, his subconscious would find the answer he sought.

He rapidly realized the fallacy of that line of thought. The scenery was depressing. A few trees were starting to come back to the Angora fire area, but much of the landscape was still stark and barren. He found himself remembering what used to be here, and how beautiful it had been. So much for letting his mind clear itself.

Jack's home was a remnant of those that had been damaged slightly. He had always been adamant about keeping defensible space around his home; in fact, he had risked a citation and fine from the Tahoe Regional Planning Agency when he arbitrarily trimmed the dead lower branches, called "ladders," off the trees on public land surrounding his property. He had defiantly taken down a dead tree adjacent to his property, without a permit. Ultimately, this action had saved his house while his neighbor, who had been afraid to risk the ire of the TRPA, lost his.

It was the neighbor's house that had sent hot ash to Jack's roof and to a juniper on the side of Jack's house. Frank's friend had learned a painful lesson when the juniper burst into flame, catching part of the house on fire. If Jack had not kept his hose ready, the damage would have been worse. Later, the Fire Departments made a point of informing the citizens that junipers were not good choices, since they were highly volatile.

Frank glided the car to the gravel covered shoulder in front of the house and stepped quickly out of the vehicle. Jack opened the door before Frank even got to the first step, a big smile spreading across the face of the older man.

"Come on in; the coffee is hot!" he gestured towards the kitchen as Frank stepped through the door.

"Smells good!" grinned Frank. As he poured a cup of hot steaming black liquid into the mug on the counter, he looked up to see Jack studying him.

"You look like you could use a little extra kick in that this morning," he said, probing Frank's eyes. "It's in the cupboard right above the pot." He kept his eyes leveled on Frank as he sipped the brew in his own hand.

"No, thanks, Jack," he sighed. "I don't need to buy any more trouble."

"Something on the case?" Jack inquired.

"No, I did something really dumb."

"Well, come on in to the war room and tell me what is going on before we tackle this murder case." The old man turned and led the way down the hall to the brightly lit room. Frank chose a recliner and settled in.

"You're looking better, Jack," he said, swallowing a big swig of the coffee.

"And you look like hell," returned Jack, "but thanks, I am doing better. Done with the chemo and my tests say I have this cancer crap on the run."

"That's really good to hear," said Frank, and meant it. He had come to realize that Jack was not only a mentor, but was one of the few close friends in his life.

"Now, spill."

Frank recounted the details surrounding the situation with Sierra. He was brutally honest about his poor decisions, clearly not looking for any sympathy. Jack listened without interruption, sipping his coffee and nodding his head from time to time. When Frank finished, he waited expectantly, not sure what Jack would say, but he was tense. He valued this man's opinion.

Jack kept him waiting while he shifted his eyes to the trees outside the window. He seemed to be watching two squirrels chasing each other around the trunk of the bigger tree, but his brow was furrowed in thought. Finally, he brought his gaze back to Frank, and nodded.

"Yes, that was a stupid thing to do." He let that hang in the air for a few seconds before he broke into a big grin. "And I would have been disappointed in you if you hadn't done it!" He laughed at the look on Frank's face. "Listen, you are a damned good cop. And part of being a good cop is sometimes you go with what your gut tells you, and the rules be damned! You know that woman is in danger and you could not turn away from that. Because of you, she has protection that could very well save her life."

Frank let out a big breath he did not realize he was holding. "Your opinion means a lot to me, Jack," he said. Jack waved off the compliment.

"Besides," Jack said with mischief in his voice, I hear she is a looker."

"How did you…?" began Frank in surprise.

"Hey, I may be old and retired, but I still have my sources!" He pointed a bony finger at Frank. "Now, let's catch this killer!"

Chapter 36

Frank presented the latest information to Jack, and the two men spent the next three hours scrutinizing the details. Sticky notes were written, posted on the board, and some moved several times. Lunch time came and they made sandwiches, then sat with beers in hand and studied the notes some more. Jack had fired up his computer and utilized the internet to look up information on distributors and retail outlets for the type of chlorine tablets that had been used in Ginger Snapper's death.

It was one thirty in the afternoon when the two men looked at each other and nodded. Frank rose and shook hands with Jack.

"Thanks for the extra set of objective eyes," he said, as he stood on the front stoop. Jack nodded, a small smile on his still too thin face. "I am going to present this to the Captain for approval before I ask for a warrant to search her house, but I expect to have the killer behind bars before the end of the day."

The drive back to the station was short, with little traffic on the road. Something was nagging at him. Nina had plenty of motive to kill Ginger, but why Stephanie? He was convinced Nina was guilty of Ginger's death, but he just couldn't get his head around how Stephanie died.

———————

"Whatcha got, Frank," asked the Captain, as the Detective walked through the door and laid a file on the desk of his superior.

"I need a search warrant for the home of Nina Roberts," he said, wasting no time. The Captain held his eyes for a few minutes, then opened the file and skimmed the contents. He bent forward, with his hand shading his forehead, in deep concentration. Frank lowered himself into a chair and waited. He knew the drill; if the Captain had questions, he would ask. Finally, he sat back and stared at Frank again.

"What do you hope to find at her home?"

"We have a sample of the chlorine tablets that killed Ginger. The sample showed a small residue of packaging that clung to the tablet. The company that made those tablets changed their packaging a month ago, and we have proof that Nina Roberts ordered a box of the tablets from this company a week before Ginger was killed."

"Couldn't these same tablets have been purchased from someone else in this area?"

"Yes, they could have, but they are so new, the two local distributors still had them in their warehouses, waiting to use up the old stock first. They just put the new stock out two days ago at one location, and yesterday for the other distributor."

"That is a strong point," nodded the Captain, tapping his pen on his desk. "And it certainly seems like the motive is solid." He chewed on his lower lip, then fixing Frank with a no nonsense look, reached for the phone. He spoke with a judge, then hung up.

"Your warrant will be ready in half an hour." He looked out at the squad room. "Take Rayburn and Ogden with you. We don't want to miss anything."

"Thanks, Captain," Frank nodded stepping out into the squad room to gather his group. He went to Rayburn first, knowing he had stayed up on the case since he watched Stephanie loaded into the ambulance. He brought him up to speed while the young cop listened attentively.

" I'm glad to be involved again, Sir," he said. "I hope we can bring the killer to justice before they can kill again."

Frank smiled. He liked this young officer. He wasn't afraid to do the right thing, as he had proven at Sierra's home that night. He was also eager to be in the middle of a tricky case.

"Do you think the killer is done?" asked Frank. He was curious to hear his thoughts. The tall, lean, young officer set his lips in a tight line as he gazed past Frank's shoulder at the wall for a minute.

"No, Sir, I don't." he replied, bringing his eyes back to meet Frank's.

"Why?" probed the Detective. He was looking for the depth and quality of the answer.

"The only apparent connection is the agency for which both these women worked," he answered. "So," he continued, more assertively, "either someone is trying to cover up a motive to kill one by killing more, or someone wants to harm the owner of the agency." He flushed slightly and looked down at his feet, then back up. "At least that is my opinion, Sir."

"Good thinking," said Frank, gracing him with a smile. "Let's get Ogden and serve that warrant."

Chapter 37

Chad answered the door, looking tired and haggard. Dressed in baggy orange lounge pants and a well worn gray sweatshirt, he looked even thinner and older than usual. He sighed and looked at each of the officers in turn before he spoke.

"What is it, Detective Riley," he asked in a voice filled with resignation.

"We have a search warrant, Mr. Roberts," said Frank, feeling a twinge of sympathy for the man.

"Well," he looked over his shoulder, hesitated, then back at Frank. "She's in that damn Jacuzzi again. Should I get her out?" Frank dashed his hopes with a nod. "Come in," Chad said, sweeping his arm, "I'll have to get a robe for her before she can get out." He shot Frank a meaningful look as he started down the hall.

"Ogden," he motioned and the young officer started after Chad. Chad stopped and looked at Frank in surprise. "I'm just going into her bedroom…" his voice trailed off.

"It's a search warrant, Chad."

"Oh. Right. Gotcha," he said quietly. He disappeared with the officer in tow and returned a minute later. He walked over to the sliding door to the patio and hesitated, turning towards Frank. "She's uh…" he gestured limply with the robe.

"Tell her we are here in case she wants to reposition herself. We are coming out with you." The three men moved closer while Chad slid the door open.

"I said leave me alone!" screeched Nina in response to the noise of the door opening.

"Nina, Detective Riley is here…" began Chad, stepping through the sliding door and onto the patio.

"How dare he! I'm not dressed!" she snarled.

The Wizard of Oz is missing their witch. The corner of Frank's mouth twitched as he fought to keep from laughing at his own thought.

Frank followed Chad out on the patio and leveled a glare at Nina, who was reclining in a sunken jacuzzi in the corner of the patio. Only her head was above the swirling water. *Thank God for jets and bubbles.* He pinched his own wrist hard – he had to stop or he would burst out laughing and lose his aura of authority.

A lattice wall encompassed three sides of the bubbling water; the open sky twinkling with stars above. The back yard beyond the patio was expansive and also surrounded by a wall, but it was much higher and made of solid wood planks. Obviously, the Roberts' valued their privacy.

"Your husband has a robe for you, Mrs. Roberts. He is going to bring it to you and you are going to put it on and get out of the tub right now."

"I will not, with you standing there!" she shouted indignantly.

"You have thirty seconds, then you are coming out of that tub with or without the robe, your choice. We will wait right here." He stood, facing the tub, hands on his hips, engaging in a battle of wills with the woman. He hoped he was reading her right; she would not make herself that vulnerable. She would not let them pull her naked from the tub; it would take away all her control, and that was important to her.

"I'll have your badge for this!" she blustered. Frank, without taking his eyes off Nina's face, reached a hand out and nudged a reluctant Chad forward.

"Twenty seconds."

Chad hurried forward and stood by the steps of the tub, the robe open wide, looking back over his shoulder with worry on his face.

"You wouldn't dare!" she hissed.

"Officers," he motioned the men out on the patio and they stood, poised to react, on either side of Chad, but still several feet back from the water. "Ten seconds," he spat.

The water splashed and Frank saw Nina's head begin to scoot over nearer to Chad. The splashing became louder as she stood, her back to the robe, the water running off her body. Chad had his eyes scrunched shut as she jammed her hands into the sleeves of the robe, jerking it closed around her body and cinching the belt tight. Chad hurriedly stepped out of the way as she stomped up the last step and stood on the patio, still dripping water. Her arms were bent at the elbows, her fists clenched tightly as she shook them at Frank.

"How dare you!" she screamed, her face livid as her voice rose in pitch. "And you let him in!" She directed her wrath at Chad now, who threw up his hands defensively and stepped back, shaking his head, shoulders slumping. She took a step towards her husband, as if to attack.

"He had no choice, unless you wanted us to break down your

front door!" Frank's voice had an icy edge to it that stopped her, and diverted her attention back to him. "Have a seat right there, Mrs. Roberts, Frank said firmly, pointing to a patio chair positioned near the outdoor fireplace in the middle of the patio.

"I need to get dressed!" she shouted, leaning her upper body forward, her hands still balled into fists as she pounded them into her thighs in anger. Her face was red and her lips twisted into an ugly snarl.

"Ogden, stay here with Mr. and Mrs. Roberts. If Mrs. Roberts is cold, Chad can turn on the fireplace. They are not to speak to each other, and Mr. Roberts should sit on the opposite side of the fireplace."

"Yes Sir!" The young man stood, hands on his duty belt, legs apart, and stared at the couple, his mouth set in a grim line. Chad took his seat immediately, but Nina walked slowly to hers, shooting daggers at the officer even after she was seated.

"Chad!" Nina yelled, swiveling her head around to glare at her husband. He jerked upright as she snapped her fingers, pointing to the fireplace. Chad merely looked at Nina, then glanced at the towering young officer, got to his feet and lit the outdoor fire. He fell back into the chair and sat, bent forward, elbows on his knees and head in his hands.

Nina sat with her arms clenched across her chest, legs crossed, and one foot swinging furiously back and forth. She glared at Chad, who had his head down, then at the officer, who returned a steely gaze of his own. She leapt to her feet and Ogden took a step towards her.

"I can't just sit here! I need to see what they are doing! I have to walk around at least!" she demanded.

"Sit down please, M'am," Ogden commanded.

"Listen to me, you little snot, "she hissed, then suddenly stopped. Ogden had simply reached around behind his belt and withdrew a pair of handcuffs, which he held up, with raised eyebrows. Huffing, she threw herself back into the chair, glaring at him. When that had no effect on the immovable face of Officer Ogden, she finally turned her eyes to the fire, and sat spitting and hissing to herself.

Chapter 38

Frank stood in the middle of Nina's bedroom, slowly scanning for anything that looked out of place. The ornate, lavish, red velvet curtains hung at windows on either side of her bed, a king sized four poster with a red satin bedspread. The nightstand yielded some prescription narcotics, which he noted were written by two different doctors, one out of state. Combined, they would be dangerously excessive. He popped them in an evidence bag and put them in his pocket.

There was a walk in closet crammed with expensive dresses and shoes, and a variety of peignoir sets hanging to one side, mostly in red. He doubted they were for Chad's benefit. He went through a dresser full of things, most of which he would rather not touch, but did.

He found two pair of sweat pants and two matching sweat shirts residing alone in the bottom drawer of the dresser. At first glance, they looked normal, but the slightly higher stack on one side of the drawer piqued his interest. The box was wrapped in the folds of one of the sweat shirts, as if the arms of the shirt were embracing the box. It was the size and shape of a file folder, but about an inch deep. It was tied with a soft, well worn, thin piece of pink ribbon. Excitement surged through him as he took the box out and carefully placed it on the bed.

"Rayburn, in here!" he called.

"Yes Sir!" he said, appearing almost like magic in the doorway. His eyes went to the box on the bed and he walked over to stand, watching as Frank untied the thin pink ribbon and lifted the lid off the box.

Baby pictures stared up at them when they cleared the lid. Frank lifted one of a smiling blonde baby girl, sitting on the lap of a younger, thinner, smiling Nina. He turned the picture over and read the name 'Justine and Mama at one year' hand written on the back. He handed it to Rayburn.

"Is that…?"

"Yes, that is Nina Roberts holding her baby," answered Frank.

"She actually has a nice smile," mused the officer. He looked at Frank. "I guess those were happier times for her."

"Yeah, I guess so," he agreed, shifting through a few more pictures before returning the lid to the box and tying the ribbon once more. He took a bigger evidence bag out of his pocket and sealed the box inside, then carried it to the living room.

"We still don't have anything that ties her to the murder or murders," said Frank thoughtfully. "Let's toss Chad's room, then take a look at the garage."

Chad had his own room, which was spartan compared to Nina's. It held a double bed with a simple blue bedspread and one nightstand and lamp. A small easy chair sat in one corner and there was a small flat screen mounted on the wall. The closet, normal in size, held a few pair of pants, a windbreaker, a few sport coats and shirts. The floor of the closet looked empty, with three pair of shoes: black and brown dress shoes and a pair of tennis shoes. A small dresser held a few sweaters, some underwear and socks. Neither his room or the attached bathroom yielded anything of interest.

"What a contrast, huh?" Frank shook his head and Rayburn nodded.

"Garage?" asked Rayburn. They had gone through the kitchen and laundry room together, even dumping out the trash and sifting through the pile. Both men walked through the living room to the kitchen and through the door into the attached garage.

A sensor light came on as they stepped through the door and faced two cars; a small, blue, Honda Accord, and a bright red Chevy Tahoe.

"Want to guess which one is hers?" asked Frank. Rayburn just grinned. "Okay, let's see if we can find some chlorine tablets."

They searched through a row of cabinets along the side of the garage, but found only tools and holiday decorations that looked like they hadn't been used in years. Next, they rummaged through the boxes under the sink in the garage.

"Hello," said Rayburn suddenly. "Didn't Stephanie die from arsenic poisoning?" He held up a small box of arsenic and pointed to a trail of white powder along the wall. Frank squinted as he used his pocket flashlight to follow the line of powder.

"Bag it," he said. "Looks like they do have mice – see the droppings?" He pointed to the tiny black points along the wall and Rayburn nodded. "But worth a comparison," finished Frank. Rayburn slipped the box into another evidence bag and stood.

"I'll take the Honda," offered Rayburn and Frank started checking through the Chevy Tahoe. After several minutes, they both stood.

"Nothing," said Rayburn. "Chad keeps his car clean."

"I didn't find anything either, except for a French fry wrapper and a used tissue tossed on the passenger side floor."   They both gave the garage another look. Suddenly, Rayburn grabbed a ladder that was leaning against the wall and climbed up to look in the rafters.

"Nothing but dust," he sighed, returning his flashlight to his duty belt. He stepped down and stacked the ladder back against the wall.

"You can smell the chlorine in that Jacuzzi as soon as you step outside," said Frank. "Where does it come from?"

He led the way back to the patio and stepped out. Chad raised his head at the sound of the door opening and met Frank's eyes. Frank crooked his finger and Chad rose quickly, then hesitated, looking from Nina to Ogden, then back to Frank. He took a step and stopped, unsure of himself as he looked to the Detective.

"Chad." Frank motioned with his hand for Nina's husband to come to him. With a worried glance back at Nina, Chad stepped forward until he stopped in front of Frank. Frank moved so Chad could enter the kitchen area, then slid the door shut. He shot a glance at Nina, and noted with some satisfaction that she started to rise, anger on her face. Ogden gave her a withering look and she sank back into her chair. He smiled to himself. *Ogden has the look down!*

"What's going on, Detective?" Frank studied his face for a few minutes, letting the tension build.

"Chad, where is the chlorine for the Jacuzzi?"

"The chlorine?" Chad looked puzzled.

"You can smell the chlorine as soon as you step out this door," Frank said, pointing to the patio. "You have complained about the smell on your wife." Chad was nodding. "So where is the chlorine kept?"

"She has a guy that comes and cleans the Jacuzzi once a week," answered Chad, "but I don't know who he is. She takes care of that, she is very picky." He gave Frank a worried look. "You'll have to ask her."

Frank ran his hand over his face, then looked out the door. He walked over to the box on the coffee table and picked it up, then strode over and stood, towering over Nina, deliberately too close for her to be able to stand with him in position. She looked at him with pure fury in her eyes.

"Get away from me!" she hissed.

He held up the box and watched her face change from fury to

terror. Her mouth slacked and she tried to grab for the box, but could not rise with Frank blocking her. She grabbed at his clothes, trying to pull herself up.

"Give me that! How did you find it!" Her voice broke and she grabbed a handful of his coat, nearly causing her to fall on the ground as he stepped back. She recovered and flung herself against him, reaching for the box. Ogden and Rayburn each took an arm and pulled her away from Frank, holding her in place.

"That's mine! You have no right! Give it back!"

"This is you, with your daughter Justine, and her father, isn't it?" The question was rhetorical; Frank already knew the answer.

"Yes! Please! Give it back!' she sobbed.

Frank watched as they lowered her into the chair again. Her arms free, she reached them out to him and begged for the return of the box. He almost felt sorry for her. Then he thought of Ginger.

"Where is the chlorine for the Jacuzzi, Mrs. Roberts?" She stared stubbornly at him now. He tapped the box against his palm; she watched every move.

"I don't know what you're talking about," she replied, "Jerry's Jacuzzi's comes by every Thursday and he cleans and services the tub."

"I'll need his number."

"Look it up, bright boy," she sneered.

"Oh." Chad said behind him. Frank turned to see Chad staring at a small statue on the patio, near the Jacuzzi.

"Chad!" warned Nina, her eyes large with frustration. "Be quiet you big fool!"

"I forgot!" He said, looking at Frank in wonder. He strode over to the statue of a frog prince and turned to Frank in triumph. "Look!" he smiled, tipping the frog's head back to reveal several small, round packages. "Chlorine." Rayburn leaned over to look in the receptacle, and then nodded at Frank. He pulled an evidence bag out a dropped the tablets inside.

"Nina Roberts, you are under arrest," Frank said.

Chapter 39

Frank sat across from Nina Roberts in the interrogation room. She was disheveled and defiant as she sat, cuffed to the table, clutching the picture of herself and Justine to her chest. Frank let her have that one picture after making a copy. It was a small, human gesture; maybe she didn't deserve it, but she was still a mother, and after wrestling with his conscience, he ultimately decided he would honor that.

He placed a tape recorder on the table and opened a file, pretending to read it while deliberately ignoring her. He almost smiled when she began drumming her finger nails on the table; even under arrest, she could not stand to be shoved aside.

"I want my own clothes!" she demanded. She grabbed a handful of the front of the orange jumpsuit she was wearing. "This is disgusting!"

"You won't need a wardrobe where you are going, Nina," he said blandly.

"You have nothing on me!" she blustered.

"I know you had a past connection to Ginger Snapper before she came to work for you," he said, laying the folder down on the table. "And we have matched the new wrapping on the chlorine tablets to the ones you had in the container on your patio." He tapped the file and she craned her neck trying to see what it said. "That's just for starters."

"I want my make up!" *She needs a hair brush, he thought.*

"Answer my questions and maybe you can get out on bail and wear what you want." He didn't think that was likely, but he was banking on her not knowing how the system worked.

"You think I'm stupid!" she sneered at him.

"We have evidence to tie you to Ginger Snapper's murder," he stated nonchalantly, locking eyes with her.

"I hated that bitch, but why would I kill her? She wasn't worth it." She tossed her head and grinned. "She was trash." She chuckled and narrowed her eyes, a darkness dancing inside them that made a shiver run up his spine.

"Wasn't she responsible for the fact you were permanently separated from your daughter?" It caught her off guard, and she reared back, her mouth open.

"What do you know about my daughter?" she hissed, her eyes

narrowing.

"She was placed in a foster home after you and her father abused her."

Nina's face twisted in a grotesque expression. Frank thought that might be one of the most evil countenances he had ever seen. He felt his stomach clench in revulsion. She leaned forward as far as the cuffs would allow.

"How do you know that? My record was sealed!"

"About that – why was your record sealed?" he said, switching tracks to keep her off balance. Her nostrils flared, followed by a sinister smile.

"I flipped on the drug dealing pig that was beating my daughter, and they sealed my record," she said triumphantly. "They gave me some cash too, stupid idiots, for being an informant. But those lying cops took my daughter away from me anyway! All I wanted was to get rid of that worthless scum, and they took her away!"

"You weren't exactly 'Mom of the Year' to your daughter either." He let that hang in the air.

Nina sat back and studied him, surprise dominating her expression. Slowly, she brought her emotions under control as she assessed her options, then set her mouth in a thin line.

"That's not true!" She was watching to see his reaction, and he knew it.

"I believe my source," he taunted.

"Ginger's dead and so is her busy body grandmother. You can't know that...unless...." Her face turned white and the color left her lips. "You know where Justine is!" she gasped. "You've talked to her! Where is she? I have to see my baby!"

"Answer my questions and I'll see what I can do." He sat perfectly still as he watched her wrestle with her thoughts.

"You bastard!" she screamed, pounding her bound hands on the table. An officer opened the door and gave Frank a questioning look, but he waved her away. The officer looked at Nina, back at Frank, and quietly closed the door to resume her watch outside the room.

For several more minutes, Frank sat stoically as Nina twisted, moaned, put her head in her hands, and pounded on the table. She even kicked the metal table leg once, and Frank almost broke his stone face to laugh when she winced in pain as the metal leg remained intact and Nina's foot obviously felt an uncomfortable twinge.

Finally, she lowered her head to the table and rested it on her hands while she swore softly, then ultimately became quiet. Frank sat, barely breathing. He knew she was mulling over her options. When she raised her head and readjusted herself in her chair, he felt oddly hopeful as she fixed him with a glittering, hate filled glare.

"If I tell you everything, you'll tell me where my daughter is?" The words were clipped, filled with resentment.

"Yes," Frank replied, as he hit the button on the tape recorder.

"Damn you!" she began. He did not move, did not take his eyes from her face. She blew out a harsh breath and flipped her head again. "That bitch had it coming."

"Ginger Snapper?" he clarified.

"Yeah, Ginger Snapper, who do you think?"

"Why?"

"I got rid of Justine's father and got my records sealed," she said, "but when I tried to get my daughter back, they told me she had been placed in a foster home and I couldn't have her back! Me! Her mother!"

"What was in your records that needed to be sealed?" She shot him a haughty look.

"I had to make a living! Her father wouldn't give me any money, so I turned a few tricks and sold a few bags. Big deal!"

"Drugs and prostitution?"

"Yeah, boy scout, what do you think I'm talking about, Einstein?" She rolled her eyes and clenched her teeth. "Those lousy cops caught me and told me they were really after Jerry, Justine's father, so I saw my chance and took it." She looked at the picture of Justine again. "And then they took my baby and put her in that home with those goody goodys."

"Did you ever try to find her again?" He was leading her and she looked at him closely, trying to determine what he was doing. After a pause, she shrugged her shoulders and answered him.

"Yeah. I found the foster home and tried to get her back." She looked away at the wall, then defiantly back at him. "But that old biddie called the cops on me and I almost went to jail."

"How did you find the foster home?" asked Frank.

"I staked out every school in the town until I saw Justine get out of a car and go into school one day. Then I followed the car home," she said proudly.

"And you tried to physically remove Justine from the home." It wasn't a question. Her eyes narrowed to slits.

"She was MY child!" she screeched. "Of course I tried to remove her, and that bitch almost got me thrown in jail!"

"How was that Ginger's fault?" he asked.

"That sniveling little brat! She held on to Justine and Justine didn't want to go with me because she had a *friend*." She said the last with a sing song whiny voice showing distain. "If it hadn't been for that little snot, my daughter would have come back to me."

Frank wisely remained silent. He doubted that the child would have chosen to go back to a home where she was abused, but he wanted more from Nina. What he had was good, but he wanted it air tight.

"Why didn't the police arrest you that day?"

"Huh!" she scoffed. "Because there was something in it for them, of course! "You think the cops ever just do something to be nice?"He waited. "They turned me into an informant again; used me just as sure as if I was on my back for them!"

"So all these years later, you decided to kill Ginger because of a childhood friendship with your daughter?"

"You are so dumb!" She flung the insult with a nasty tone in her voice. "No, I tried to get in touch with Justine, sending her cards all those years at *Granny Goody's* house, but they were always returned unopened." She looked down at the table and sat silent for a few minutes. Frank waited.
"I thought all I had to do was stick it out until Justine graduated high school." She fiddled with the cuffs on her wrists, and studied the tile on the floor. "But Ginger still had a hold on my baby girl, and Justine didn't want anything to do with me." Nina wiped her nose on her hand.

"What happened after she graduated?"

"She was still at Ginger's, so I started calling every day. I even showed up once, but she wouldn't talk to me. Then one day, she was just gone, and I couldn't find her." Her eyes glistened with moisture as she looked at Frank. "I watched every day for a week, but she never came back."

"How did you find Ginger after all this time?" asked Frank, leaning forward to hear the answer.

"That's the funniest thing of all!"She actually hooted and Frank felt a chill. "That stupid little bitch walked right through my door one day, looking for a job!"

"Didn't she recognize you?"

"No, I had a different last name because I married that loser Chad. My hair is red now and it used to be a dirty blonde. I'm a little heavier, you know, getting a little older does that," she said defensively. "She was just a little brat when she met me. But I recognized her because I had watched her with Justine, sitting outside the different schools as she grew up, just to catch a glimpse of my own daughter!" Nina stared into space and seemed to go to another place in her mind. Frank waited. Suddenly, she jerked upright and brought herself back to the moment. "And that name! Ginger Snapper! How could I forget that!"

"You employed her, knowing who she was?" asked Frank. His stomach was churning as he listened to the cold calculation. *Keep your poker face on!*

"Of course! It was perfect! She stepped right into the spider's web and I knew I could toy with her and teach her a lesson!"

"It must have been hard to get into her apartment," he probed. He felt sick to his stomach, but he had her talking and he didn't want to lose his edge.

"Ha ha ha! It was so easy! Our application asks for their home address, so I sat and watched her apartment several times, and twice I noticed when the wind blew even a little, the back door would sometimes come open." She grinned.

"Seems like that would be kind of hit or miss – like you couldn't count on the door coming open."

"Duh!" She rolled her eyes. "There's this thing called a weather report – ya know, it tells you when it's going to be windy, smart guy!"

"Still a gamble," he said, ignoring her cutting comment.

"I'm not stupid! One day I was so angry with her and what she had done, it was eating at me; I just couldn't get it out of my head. Even the Jacuzzi couldn't relieve my tension. I blew up at her at work, and Chad grabbed her and took her away. Off to some motel, I found out later. Tramp!" she sniffed. "But I had a key to her locker, and after everyone left, I got her keys from the locker and made a copy of her house key," she cackled. "She never noticed!"

"That was really clever!" He flattered her and got the desired result.

"And then, when I decided to do it, I assigned her to a delivery in Truckee, over an hour's drive away." She giggled and it was somehow an obscene sound. "Then I gave her another assignment right after, so she wouldn't go home until later. I made sure she had to wear the plastic head so she would be hot and want a shower." Her eyes glittered. "I watched her leave, and then went in and fixed up that bathroom real good."

"How did you know what to do?" He was disgusted by her apparent glee at murdering Ginger, but he wanted to get the whole story.

"You aren't too bright, are you?" Frank felt the color rise in his neck and up into his face, but he kept still. "Justine's daddy was a plumber, at least when he worked. He made me go along to do his odd jobs with him, and I learned things." She grinned wickedly. "But I also learned I could slip out later and make some real money in a lot less time if I went back without Jerry, if you know what I mean." She winked at him and leered as her eyes traveled up and down his body.

I'm going to need a shower myself when I am done here. He tapped his fingers on the table, shifted his eyes to the door, and brought them back hard on her.

"Just tell me the story if you want to know where your daughter is now." His voice was hard and his eyes icy.

"What are you a virgin or something?" Nina sat up and shifted in her chair, tossing her head. "You don't know what you're missing."

Frank stood, picked up the tape recorder, and started for the door. Nina jumped to her feet, knocking the chair over and catching herself on the cuffs binding her to the table.

"Wait! Where are you going? Where is my daughter? You promised!" she shrieked.

"No, I said I would tell you where she is after you tell me how you killed Ginger. I have no interest in playing games with you." He put his hand on the door handle and started to open the door, his back to her.

"No! I'll tell you everything!" He stood in the doorway and smiled at the officer outside the door. She smiled back, a twinkle in her eye. "Please!"

Frank turned and faced her, crossing his arms over his chest. "We have already tied the chlorine tablet packaging we found at your house to the ones used to kill Ginger. He stared at her, his mouth set. "Give me a good reason to come back and sit down." Silently, he was patting himself on the back. He picked the recorder up, but he hadn't turned it off.

"I switched out her inhaler too!" She was desperate now.

"How?" he demanded. He made no move towards the table.

"She threw an empty one in the trash one day, and I snagged it.

When I went in her apartment, I took the good one out of the medicine cabinet and left her the empty one." She laughed, and Frank fought to keep the contents of his stomach down.

He stood, watching her for another few minutes, letting the tension build. He sauntered back to the table and sat down, once more placing the recorder on the table between them, but out of her reach.

"Why did you kill Stephanie?" he asked.

"I didn't kill her, and you promised to tell me where my daughter is now!"

"We know you killed her too," he bluffed, "but we don't know why yet."

"I didn't kill her, and you can't prove I did! Now where is my daughter, I need to get in touch with her! I need to see her; she will understand if I can just explain!" Frank stood and stepped towards the door. "You promised!" Nina screeched.

At the door, Frank turned and faced the sullen woman. "Your daughter is in the north west, and she does not want to see you." He watched her face morph from shock to anger.

"Where in the north west?" she demanded. "I need to find her!" Nina pounded on the table for emphasis.

"She doesn't want to see you. She was here to claim Ginger's body and she made it perfectly clear she wants nothing to do with you. In fact, she made me promise I would never tell you where she is. I told you the part of the country she is in; I never promised to tell you exactly where she is." It was mean, and somewhat dishonest, but he justified it as he looked at the depraved woman before him.

"Liar! You bastard!" she screamed, rising again until the cuffs stopped her.

Frank closed the door on her yelling, and walked to his Captain's office.

Chapter 40

His Captain walked with him to the observation room and stood beside him, watching her for a few moments.

"She confessed?"

"She finally admitted killing Ginger Snapper. She had a lot of pent up anger towards her, and believes Ginger is the reason she did not get her daughter back."

The Captain nodded. "So the chlorine tablet wrapper matched the one on the tablets that killed Ginger?"

"Yes, and she had ample access to Ginger's inhaler." He turned to the Chief. "She calculated everything. She is one malicious and cold woman." Frank shook his head. "She glued the window shut and tampered with the lock on the bathroom door."

"How did she get in Ginger's apartment?" asked the Captain. Frank recounted the rest of the story while the superior officer stood, listening.

"I believe we have enough on her to charge her with Ginger Snapper's murder," said Frank.

"What about Stephanie?" asked the Captain, why did she kill her?"

"That's just it. She still says she had nothing to do with Stephanie's murder."

"I thought you found arsenic in her garage?"

"We did," Frank shrugged, "but there is nothing special about this box. We found they do have mice in the garage, and arsenic is a common method for killing rodents, even though it is not used much these days. We can't tie her to that one."

"She broke pretty fast on this one; do you think if we keep working her she will admit she killed the other woman too?"

"I don't know," Frank sighed. "She wanted something from us on Ginger's murder; she was hoping to get another chance with her daughter and she thought she could manipulate us into making that happen." He shivered involuntarily. "I believe she is truly vile, but there doesn't seem to be any motive for the other woman's murder." He chewed on his lower lip. He looked at his Captain. "I can't shake the feeling I am missing something."

"Well, keep stewing on it then, but for now, charge her with Ms.

Snapper's murder and let's get it to trial," said the Captain, slapping Frank on the arm.

"Yes Sir," Frank responded. Something was bothering him, but what? He stayed for several minutes after the Captain left, watching Nina as she rocked back and forth, holding the picture.

Chapter 41

Frank walked over to the ME building, hands in his pockets and head down. He hadn't been in the building since the issue with Sierra O'Malley, but he wanted to talk to Bruce. The young man looked up as Frank walked in.

"Hey Frank! Long time, no see," he said with a smile.

"Yeah. I thought it best to stay away from here for awhile," he shrugged.

"I heard," said Bruce balefully. "If it's any consolation, she seems to be less jumpy and has a little color in her cheeks these days."

"Keeping her safe was my first thought." Silence sat between them for a few moments. "Anything new on that arsenic? The sample we brought in from the Roberts' garage?"

"I thought at first it was pretty generic, but I was just looking over the file again. Funny thing..." began Bruce and then stopped. "It might be nothing."

"What did you find?" asked Frank, sitting forward in his chair.

"I missed it at first, but the arsenic on the garage floor was a different form of arsenic than what was in the box," said Bruce.

"I don't follow," said Frank, shaking his head.

"The arsenic on the floor was organic arsenic, but what was in the box was inorganic."

"I thought all arsenic was the same?" Frank raised his eyebrows, puzzled.

"Not quite," said Bruce. "Organic arsenic is generally used as a pesticide because it is not as fast acting. That would be desirable if you were poisoning something like mice, because you would want them to go back to their nest to die. It is also unlikely they will drink water right away to dilute the arsenic, so it is great for rodent control."

"How is that different from inorganic arsenic?"

"Inorganic arsenic is more rapidly absorbed into the system and results in a faster death." Bruce paused, then looked Frank straight in the eye. "Stephanie was killed with inorganic arsenic."

Frank stared at Bruce, digesting what he had just been told. "So why would both types be at the Roberts house?"

"That's a really good question," said Bruce. Frank started to rise, but Bruce stopped him. "One more thing, Frank."

"What's that?" he asked, pausing mid rise.

"For the past several years, arsenic of all types has been discouraged as a use for pest control. It is more difficult to get than it used to be."

"Who can get arsenic, and where then? Can it still be bought over the counter?"

"It's used in pyrotechnics, some ammunition manufacturing, and some electronics, but rarely as a pesticide anymore. The sample from the Roberts garage floor was older than that in the box you brought in."

"But what does all this mean?" Frank wondered out loud.

"That's why you are the Detective and I am just a lab guy," shrugged Bruce.

"Thanks!" he laughed. "Thanks a lot," he said distractedly. *Now why the hell was this important?*

Chapter 42

Frank put in a call to Jack and was on his way to the former ME's home when his radio blasted a call that had him turning around. There was a 911 call for Sierra O'Malley's address; someone attempting to break in the house. He hadn't asked if she was home today, but it didn't matter. Frank was five minutes away and responded.

"Dispatch, this is Detective Frank O'Malley, I am in the vicinity and will respond. Repeat, I am responding."

"Ten four. Be advised another unit is on the way."

"Copy that," replied Frank, stepping on the gas and turning corners faster than he should. Sierra's house came into his view and there was a large man on the steps. As he approached, he saw the man kick the door in and race inside.

Frank's car careened to a stop across the shoulder, hemming in the car at the side of the road. *At least he will have to back up before he can get away.*

Frank jumped out of his vehicle, not bothering to shut the door. Cautiously, he cleared his weapon as he heard screams and yelling coming from the home. He ran to the door, then peered around the edge, advancing with weapon drawn, towards the back of the house where the shouting intensified.

"Give me the boy!" yelled a man, whose voice seemed close.

"Get out of this house!" returned another man, then sounds of scuffling and a woman's scream reached his ears. A child began to cry, and Frank came around the corner to see two men struggling, while an older woman huddled in a corner, cradling a boy Frank guessed to be about five years old. One look told him this had to be Garrett.

"I want the child! It is my right!" shouted the younger man, reaching in his coat and withdrawing a hunting knife. The older man fell back, holding both hands in front of him as he retreated. Suddenly the gray haired man grabbed a dining chair from under the counter separating the kitchen and dining area, and held it in front of him.

"Miriam, get Garrett out the back door!" The woman rose, and shielding the boy, edged behind the man with the chair.

"Police! Drop the knife!" Frank shouted. For a moment, no one moved, then all eyes turned towards him. Suddenly, the younger man grabbed a leg of the chair and yanked, pulling the older man off balance.

"John!"screamed Miriam, as her husband fell forward on the floor and hit his head on the tile.

"Grandpa!" cried the little boy as the younger man ducked around an end of the kitchen counter and wrestled with Miriam for the child. He still held the knife in one hand, but Frank did not have a clear shot.

"Drop the knife! Frank repeated, leveling his gun at the assailant as he advanced around the opposite end of the counter.

"George!" cried Sierra, running into the dining area. "Get away from my son! Get out of my house!" Frank held one hand out to signal she should stay back, but Sierra disregarded the motion and ran the opposite way around the counter.

"Sierra, stop!" commanded Frank. She faltered and looked between the two men, uncertainty spreading over her features.

"Mom!' cried Garrett, wresting free of Miriam's grasp and starting towards his mother.

But George quickly scooped Garrett up and held him against his chest, grinning wickedly as he sidled towards the back door, the knife poised at the child's throat. Frank couldn't risk the shot. He holstered his gun and advanced slowly towards George.

"You can't get away," he said calmly, hearing the siren getting closer. "Drop the knife and put the boy down." He was slowly stepping closer, but George was still backing up. Frank was waiting. At some point, George would have to release the boy or lower the knife to open the back door.

"If I can't have him, maybe I'll send him to his father," George said calmly. Too calmly. Frank did not like the crazed look in his eyes.

"No!" gasped Sierra, "please don't hurt him!"

George came up against the door, and surveyed the room. Indecision shown on his face; he was trying to figure out how to open the door without losing any ground.

"Back off!" he shouted at Frank. "Get back now or I swear I will cut him!" He brandished the knife in Frank's direction as he spoke.

Suddenly, there was a loud knock at the door behind George. He whirled, and Garrett kicked him hard in the stomach, then wrenched himself free to fall to the floor. George was caught between reaching for the boy and trying to watch the back door. Frank lunged for him just as the back door burst open, knocking George forward.

Frank twisted and grabbed the knife arm, sending an elbow into

George's stomach. As the man slumped forward, Frank brought his knee up and smashed George's forearm against his thigh. George howled in pain as the knife clattered to the floor.

Rayburn stepped into the room and kicked the knife out of reach, then helped wrestle the man to the floor. He grinned at Frank as he slapped hand cuffs on George and hauled him to his feet.

"Great timing," said Frank.

"I could hear everything through the door," replied Rayburn. I wanted to make a big impression!"

"Well, you sure did that!" laughed Frank. "Smart move; he wasn't expecting a knock!"

"Mind if I put this guy in the back of the unit, Detective?" Rayburn beamed, pushing George towards the back door.

"Be my guest!" Frank nodded with a smile. He surveyed the room and saw John sitting in a chair with Miriam dabbing at a small cut on his forehead. John shook his head up and down at Frank, and the Detective turned his eyes on the two figures sitting on the floor. He stepped over to Sierra, who sat, rocking Garrett in her lap.

"Is he alright?" he asked, kneeling down to look at the boy. Large green eyes, wide with excitement, stared back at Frank from under a tousled head of short, black hair. Garrett raised his head off his Mom's shoulder and looked at Frank.

"Mom said if anyone ever grabbed me, I should kick him!" offered Garrett.

"That's good advice, "Frank said to the boy, "and you did very well!"

"Mom, he has a gun," said Garrett soberly, studying Frank. "Is he a policeman?" asked the young child.

"Yes," Sierra answered her son, "the police are our friends." She caught Frank's eyes and held them for a minute with the warmth of her smile.

"Why don't you introduce us to this nice man?" interjected Miriam.

"Oh," responded Sierra, "Detective Riley, these are my parents, Miriam and John Brogan." Pleasantries were exchanged, and thanks received. Frank asked for and received, assurances that John was truly not harmed.

"I am glad your parents are here to help," said Frank, looking from one to the other.

"When we heard Sierra was being stalked again, we came right away," said John. "We have been discussing moving here anyway. We are both retired and Garrett is our only grandchild, so why not?" said John, putting his arm around the waist of a smiling Miriam.

"Detective, do you think they will keep George locked up for awhile," asked Miriam. Frank could see the fear in her eyes.

"We will have to see what the judge says, but there is a good chance that is what will happen,: answered Frank truthfully. *If he had anything to say about it, he would put George away for a long time.*

"Why don't you come back for dinner tomorrow night," asked Miriam, giving Frank an impish smile.

"She's a good cook!" enticed John.

Frank searched Sierra's face for his answer, and got a nod from her. "That would be great," he answered.

"Six o'clock, then," said Miriam, matter of factly.

"Thank you, M'am. I better go finish up the arrest now," he said, taking his leave.

Chapter 43

Frank followed Rayburn back to the station, gave his account of the incident, and made sure George was behind bars, and would stay there awhile. He turned to Rayburn and clapped him on the shoulder.

"Great police work!" he said as the younger officer smiled. "Quick thinking on your entrance! He might have been expecting the door to open if he heard the sirens, but even I wasn't expecting you to knock! That really threw him!"

"Thanks, Detective, I was just thinking on my feet, Sir!"

"Well, keep doing that! You're a good cop, Rayburn; definitely an asset to the department."

He left the young officer still smiling from the compliment, and walked to the parking lot. *Reminds me of myself when I was younger.* He laughed out loud.

For the second time that day, he wove his car through the streets towards Jack's house. It was already mid afternoon when he pulled up to the modest home and walked up the steps. Once again, Jack opened the door before he knocked.

"Well, glad you could make it!" he chided.

"Duty calls!" retorted Frank with humor. "Sounds like you miss being in the middles of all the excitement, old man!" Both men laughed.

"Seeing you and hashing out a case is all the excitement I can handle these days!" Jack chortled. "And watch that 'old man' stuff; I'm getting stronger every day! I'll be running circles around you soon!" He walked into the kitchen, then eyed Frank. "How is the lovely ME?" he teased.

"Safe! At least I think so for now. The stalker is in jail, and the evidence is pretty solid, so not likely he will be released before his court date. Judges take a dim view of holding a knife to the throat of a child."

"You said something about family when you called to say you would be late; someone is helping her?" clarified Jack.

"Yes, I met her mother and father. They are staying with her for now, at least."

"Ah! Meeting the parents already, huh?" Jack jabbed.

"It's not like that!" protested Frank. To his chagrin, he felt himself coloring.

Jack stepped back and studied the detective. Frank was avoiding his gaze. After several uncomfortable minutes, Jack grinned. "You are going back," he stated.

"Well," started Frank, shifting from one foot to the other, "her Mom invited me back for dinner tomorrow night." He looked at the counter, peering from under his eyebrows at Jack.

The former ME's body started to shake. Then he turned his back to Frank and bent over. Frank straightened and took a step towards the man, laying his hand on his arm.

"Jack! Are you alright?" He was met with a burst of laughter!

"You lucky son of a gun!" guffawed the older man. "You nearly lose your shield because of a woman, and now you are going to dinner at her house?" He was laughing so hard tears were running down his cheeks now. "Only you!"

Frank was grinning sheepishly now. "Hey, I did catch the bad guy!"

"And you are having dinner with her parents!" He blew his nose and tried to control the laughter. He cleared his throat, looked at Frank, and had to suppress a giggle. He shook his head. "Okay, Romeo, let's get to work and clean up this case."

It felt good to be bantering with Jack; just like old times. His long time friend was looking better and stepping more lively than when he had first found him after the ME retired. Even though he was the brunt of the joke, it had felt wonderful to hear his friend bubbling with laughter. Frank breathed a sigh of relief. He had missed his friend, and like many things in life, he had taken Jack's friendship for granted until it was no longer readily available.

Jack grabbed two cold beers and a bag of Sun Chips and led the way down the hall. They settled in their respective favorite chairs, and Frank filled Jack in on the latest developments. Jack listened intently, staring at the wall, as was his custom when processing something complicated. He once told Frank that looking at 'white space" cleared his mind of all distractions so he could listen more carefully.

"I had forgotten about the differences in arsenic," Jack nodded. "It doesn't come into play as much anymore."

"I just can't shake the feeling that this isn't over yet," said Frank.

"I agree," said Jack slowly. "Something doesn't feel right. Why would the Roberts have more than one kind of arsenic?"

"Unless someone set them up," said Frank, looking at Jack for confirmation. Jack nodded in agreement.

"What does your gut say about Nina Roberts? Do you think she did both of the murders?" asked Jack.

"No," replied Frank slowly. "She is a real cold one, and I think I have a solid case for Ginger, but Stephanie...I can't make it work."

"Any other leads?"

"I wish," said Frank. "I am having trouble with both motive and opportunity. One of them needs to open up for me!"

"Keep on it. Something will break if you stay focused." Jack stroked his chin. "I agree though, something is off and I think there is more to come."

"Yeah," Franks said, blowing out a breath and staring out the window. Finally, he shook his head and shrugged his shoulders in Jack's direction. "I just hope I can figure it out before someone else gets hurt or worse. I can't shake this feeling of foreboding."

"Trust your instincts, Frank, they are good. You'll worry it out."

His friend looked tired, and not wanting to drain his energy too much, Frank nodded, picked up the half empty beer bottles, and took them back to the kitchen on his way out. Home sounded awful good.

Chapter 44

Frank didn't even make it to his desk the next morning before the Captain was leaning out of his office door, waving at him to hurry.

"Frank," said the Captain. "There has been an attempted murder, and it involves an employee at "We do it Your Way.""

The detective stood rooted to the spot in front of the Captain's desk. *Damn it. I have a killer in custody* he thought, as he stared at the Chief in disbelief. "Who is it?" he asked, when he could find his voice.

"Michelle Cassin," he replied. "One of the delivery …options." He knit his brows together, not quite sure of her actual job title. "She was just taken by ambulance to the hospital with some kind of poison suspected."

"Ambulance – so she is still alive?" Frank asked.

"Yes." The Captain hesitated, then spoke. "It sounds like it could be related to your case, so get on over to the hospital and see what you can find out."

No reply was needed; Frank wheeled and was out the door at a fast walk. He remembered the woman from the first day he walked into the office of the delivery service. She was arguing with Chad when he walked in, then she walked out, past Ken, almost immediately. *Did he miss something?*

He chewed on his lip as he drove to the other end of town and pulled into the parking area behind the hospital. Moving quickly, he went in the side door reserved for ambulance admittance, and swept past the exam rooms, glancing in as he moved by, until he saw a nurse he recognized.

"Linda," he said, "did they just bring in a young woman named Michelle Cassin?"

"Good to see you again too, Frank," she laughed. Two more rooms down on the left," she pointed.

"Thanks!" he called over his shoulder as he rapidly closed the distance to the room. He stopped at the doorway and looked in to see a doctor standing at her bedside, writing in a chart. Michelle lay on the bed, eyes closed, and skin as pale as the white sheet on which she lay.

The doctor looked up, and asked a question by lifting his eyebrow. Frank flashed his shield, and the unspoken conversation continued as the doctor nodded.

"Is she…" asked Frank.

"No, she is just resting," replied the doctor, walking towards Frank. "Let's step out in the hall."

"Poison of some kind?" asked Frank, keeping his voice low and standing a few feet from the door to the room.

"Yes," he answered, "at least it certainly appears to be a reaction to some kind of poison, but I can't identify what it is."

"What symptoms did she present?"

"Seizures, vomiting, and unresponsive." He nodded as two orderlies came into the room and put the sides of the bed up. They began to wheel her out the door. "I'm waiting for lab work, but she seems to be stable for now."

"Will I be able to talk to her?" asked Frank. The doctor shook his head.

"Not for a few hours. I am moving her into a room so we can keep an eye on her, but I don't expect her to be lucid for several hours."

"Who called 911?" asked Frank.

"I think her boyfriend, but you would have to double check that. We couldn't let him in the room with her since she came in unresponsive and he is not a relative. He might be in the waiting room." A siren screamed within hearing. "Excuse me, Detective, I have another patient," he said, turning to the doors as another ambulance arrived.

Frank walked through the double doors into the ER waiting room and surveyed the people sitting around the room. A young man was bent forward, elbows on his knees, head down, rocking.

"Excuse me," said Frank, standing in front of him. The man sat back and looked up at Frank, wiping his eyes with the palms of his hands. "Did you come in with Michelle?"

"Yeah," he nodded, his brown eyes moist. "Is she alright?"

"I'm Detective Riley," said Frank, showing the man his badge. "Could we talk?"

"Sure. Chris Campbell," he said, standing and automatically offering his hand. His hand shake was strong, and Frank noted the corded muscles in his arms. "Is she ok?" he repeated. "They haven't told me anything." He jammed his hands into the pockets of his jeans. He was a couple of inches shorter than Frank's six two, and leaner, yet still muscular. His dark brown hair was shaved close up the sides, with a longer cut above his ears. Frank pegged him as late twenties, and judging by his physical strength, possibly someone who worked in the construction trades.

"They just moved her to a room to watch her," he answered. "The doctor said she is stable, at least for now." He didn't see the harm in sharing that information. "Are you the one that called it in?"

"Yeah. We were supposed to meet for lunch, but she didn't show and didn't answer her phone, so I drove over." He stared at the floor, seeming to be in a trance.

"Where did you find her?" prompted Frank.

"In the bathroom. The door was open and she was like, on the floor, twitching. There was some vomit. Must have happened suddenly, she knocked some make up and other stuff on the floor."

"Had she ever had convulsions before?"

"I don't think so," he said, looking at Frank in surprise, like it hadn't occurred to him until now. "We've been dating for a few months, and I never saw it before. She never mentioned it." He looked at Frank with sad eyes. "Is she really going to be alright?"

"I'm not a doctor," he replied, "but if they are moving her to a room, it is a good sign." The young man nodded. "Did you see anything on the floor or counter that was unusual? Was she taking any medication?"

"No, I don't think so. The medicine cabinet was open, but all I saw was some cosmetics, you know mascara, stuff like that, some aspirin, and I think a bottle of eye drops. I didn't see anything that could hurt her." He shifted from foot to foot, and glanced at the outer door before returning his gaze to Frank. "I mean, neither of us does drugs or anything." He stared straight into Frank's eyes, almost challenging him to dispute the information.

"Could you show me where she lives? Maybe if I take a look I can see something you missed."

Chris studied Frank's face, clearly torn. "Well, it's not my apartment," he said slowly. "I mean, I know you are a cop and all, but can I really give you permission to go into someone else's home?"

"No, you can't," smiled Frank. "It would just help if you could show me where she lives. I can find out, but it would save me some time, and that might be helpful for the doctor if I find something." Chris didn't move. "Maybe it would help if you just gave me the address. I can get the manager to let me in."

"I'll show you," he said suddenly, making a decision. "Especially if it will help her. I just don't want to do anything wrong." He shrugged his shoulders in a helpless gesture.

"You are right to ask questions," Frank assured him, "and I appreciate the help."

Chris nodded, and casting a look in the direction of the doors to the treatment rooms, he led the way to the parking lot. He climbed into a truck with Chris Campbell Cabinets written on the side, and waited until Frank was behind him before he pulled out.

Chapter 45

Frank didn't have to bother the manager when he got to the apartment; she was already standing in the doorway with Rayburn. Chris looked relieved that he was not the one breaching Michelle's privacy, and visibly relaxed as Frank and Rayburn shook hands.

"You beat me here," grinned Frank.

"Yeah," the younger officer responded sheepishly. I heard a possible poisoning going out over the radio and since I was just a couple of blocks away, I thought I'd keep busy." He shrugged, then gestured to the tall, slender woman standing just inside the doorway. "This is Grace Burrows, the manager."

"I'm Detective Riley," Frank said, nodding.

"Nice to meet you, Detective," she smiled, the warmth in her brown eyes genuine. She dipped her head in his direction, then shifted her gaze to Chris. "Are you okay? What happened?"

"I'm fine, Mrs. Burrows," he said, "I'm just worried about Michelle."

"I bet you are, honey," she soothed, "me too." Frank smiled at her motherly concern, readily accepted by the young man. He wished he could call her from time to time to be a comfort in some of the other cases they had to handle. "What can we do to help?" Grace asked, splitting her attention between the two officers.

"We'd like to look around to see if we can find any answers." Frank hesitated, then glanced at Rayburn before he spoke again. "Michelle worked for an agency where there have been other ...accidents," he said, choosing his words carefully.

Chris and Grace stood staring at them, as if they did not quite understand. Then Grace took Chris' arm and steered him towards the door.

"I live next door," she called over her shoulder, "we'll be back in a few minutes with some coffee and sandwiches." They disappeared through the opening and Rayburn and Frank put on plastic gloves.

"I'll take the bathroom," said Frank. "Chris said that is where he found her." He moved towards a lighted doorway off the hall.

"I'll check the kitchen," Rayburn added, walking through the arch between the two rooms.

Frank stood in the door of the bathroom, surveying the scene before stepping in. Chris was right; it looked like she fell suddenly, sending random items to the floor as she went down. A tube of mascara, with the brush laying a foot from it, was on the floor, as well as a bottle of aspirin and a bottle of eye drops, missing a cap. His attention was drawn to a cup of what looked like orange juice, sitting on the bathroom counter, against the splash back.

It was nearly empty, but he withdrew a small dropper and plastic container from his pocket, and secured a sample in the container. He emptied the minute amount remaining into the sink, and placed the cup in a separate plastic bag.

He scooped all the cosmetics he saw into a bag, then put the eye drop container in another. Emptying the waste basket into a larger bag, he saw nothing else of interest. Rayburn appeared in the hall.

"Nothing unusual in the kitchen, but I took samples of open food stuffs just the same." He held up a plastic bag tied at the top. "This is the trash from the kitchen," he added, dropping the bag by the front door. "Bedroom?"

Frank nodded and the two men searched the bedroom, to no avail. Nothing indicated poison.

"Hungry?" called Mrs. Burrows from the living room.

"Reminds me of my Mom," grinned Rayburn.

Mrs. Burrows had a carafe of coffee and a plate of sandwiches. Chris carried a tray with paper plates, ceramic coffee mugs, napkins, and cream and sugar for the coffee. They set the lunch down on a coffee table and everyone took a seat.

"Mrs. Burrows," began Frank, after most of the sandwiches had been consumed.

"Grace, please," she smiled, "I tolerate the 'Mrs.' from Chris because I am old enough to be his mother, but you, not so much!" she laughed.

"Ok, Grace," Frank started again, a grin spreading across his face. "Is there anything you can tell us about Michelle? Anyone hanging around the apartments lately that didn't belong? Any visitors?"

"Other than Chris?" she asked. "No, Michelle was not a party person, she didn't have a lot of visitors. She went to work, came home, went out with Chris, that's all I know."

"How did you meet Michelle?" asked Rayburn, turning to Chris.

"I have a cabinet making business," he beamed. "Mrs. Burrows asked me to replace the cabinets in the kitchen and well, Michelle was home and we hit it off." Silence settled on their thoughts, and Frank looked at Rayburn.

"Here's my card," said Frank, handing one to each of them. "Let us know if you think of anything else." He and Rayburn rose to leave. "Thank you for the sandwiches, Grace," he smiled. He turned half way to the door. "One more thing, Grace, could you please lock the apartment up for now and don't let anyone in?"

"Of course, Detective." She locked the door as they watched, then walked to her apartment.

Chris stood outside the apartment looking forlorn as he stared at Michelle's door. He looked at the officers. "Can I go back to the hospital now? In case she wakes up?"

"I don't see why not," answered Frank. "We'll be in touch as soon as we know anything." Chris nodded, then walked to his truck. Frank felt sorry for the young man.

Rayburn climbed back in his unit, nodding at Frank as he drove away. Frank had work to do.

Chapter 46

Frank wanted to get the evidence in to Bruce before he drove back to the hospital. He walked through the doors with two plastic bags; one holding the smaller evidence bags, the other the contents of the waste basket.

"I just love when you bring me presents!" Bruce snickered as Frank deposited the two bags on the man's desk.

"You want flowers next time?" he bantered.

"That would be great! I could take them home and make points with my wife!" Bruce laughed, then glanced down the hall. "Sierra took today off. I thought she was doing better, but she got a call yesterday and tore out of here at a dead run. I haven't been able to get any details, except that they caught the guy that was stalking her."

"Oh, sorry Bruce," apologized Frank. "I feel like such a heel! I was going to fill you in this morning, but I got pulled away." He grabbed a chair and sat down to bring the assistant ME up to speed.

"Wow! So our instincts were right – she was in danger." He stared at Frank. "If you had not trusted your instincts, she could be dead and her little boy in the hands of a mad man."

"Hey, you tipped me off, partner!"Frank clapped him on the arm. Bruce nodded, then fractured the serious look on his face with a broad smile.

"The Dynamic Duo!" he grinned with mischief in his eyes.

"Or not," groaned Frank, rising from his chair. He glanced at the clock on the wall. "I'm headed back to see if Michelle can tell me anything. Let me know right away if you find anything."

———————

Michelle was sitting up in bed when Frank walked in the room. Chris was by her side, looking concerned. She had a little color in her cheeks now.

"Ms. Cassin, I'm Detective Riley," he began, flashing the obligatory badge. "Are you up to answering a few questions?"

"Sure," she said, scooting up a little higher in the bed.

"When did you first realize you felt sick? Did you feel something was wrong?" Frank pulled out his notebook and a pen, poised to take notes, but watching her face at the same time.

"A few days ago. I was at work." She hesitated, and looked down at her lap, kneading her hands together. "Nina and Chad were in the break room, whispering." She looked up at him with misty eyes, one tear slowly rolling down her cheek.

"Could you hear what they were saying?" Frank wasn't sure where this was going, but he was going to play it and see. He was wondering why she started at that point, with Chad and Nina.

"They were talking about Stephanie," she sniffed, "then Chad said all he did was buy the arsenic for the mice." She sobbed into both hands and Chris stood, beside her, gently patting her back.

"Did they know you were there?" asked Frank, studying her carefully.

"Yes!" she cried. "I was so scared, they both stopped talking when they saw me standing there. At first, they just stared at me. I was uneasy, and said excuse me, I didn't know anyone was in the room. I smiled and walked out, but…"she threw her hands in the air. "They knew I heard them!" A sob escaped her lips and Chris put his arm around her shoulders.

"Did they say anything to you?"

"No. They were in the break room for another ten minutes, but I couldn't hear anything else. I sat in the main room with Celeste, trying to act like nothing had happened."

"So, exactly when did you start to feel ill?" he probed.

"Well, they came out of the break room and Nina and Chad were acting really happy. Nina said things had been tense, but that we were like family to her, and they were going to get some food to let us know how much they appreciate us." She took a deep breath and looked at Chris, who gave her a reassuring smile.

"You're doing fine, honey," he said, obviously trying to help her relax.

" They said we were the only employees they had left and they wanted to do a little something to thank us for our loyalty," she continued.

Why is she laying out this back story? Frank' antenna was up – something didn't jell here.

"Ken doesn't work there anymore?" asked Frank. He was not really surprised, but he was trying to get the players straight in his mind.

"No," said Michelle, shaking her head. "He came in about a week ago and said he just couldn't get over what happened to Ginger and Stephanie. He quit."

"So they bought you lunch?" He stared at her, trying to understand the point.

"Yeah, but they didn't take us out. They said we had to stay and answer the phone, so Nina went and got some Chinese food and served us all." Michelle shook her head, wiping away a tear.

"You're doing great, Michelle," said Chris, giving her a big smile. He held her hand in his and received a limp smile in return.

"I thought it was a little over salted, but I ate it anyway because I was trying to act normal."

"Did you start to feel sick after you ate the food?" asked Frank, still trying to organize what she was saying.

"Not until later that night. I just thought I was getting the flu or something. But then I remembered Nina sent leftovers home with me, and I ate them that night."

"Are you suggesting they may have put something in the food?"

"Well, it came on and didn't go away. Yesterday, I stopped by the office and told them I couldn't work because I felt a little sick. Nina gave me some special tea she makes for us when we are sick. She said she didn't want me to get sick, she was down to just me and Celeste."

"Nina gave you tea and food in the past two days?"

"Yeah. Just seems kinda weird she would give me stuff to eat and drink and then I get sick." Her eyes were big as she implored him to understand.

"Okay, thanks for answering my questions," he said. "Are you going home soon?"

"Yes," answered Chris. "I'm going to take her in about an hour."

"I hope you feel better," he said as he closed his notebook. He left the couple talking quietly. The puzzle was shifting into place.

Chapter 47

Frank opened the door to "We Do it Your Way" and was surprised to hear laughter. Celeste and Chad both turned at the sound; the smiles freezing on their faces.

"Detective Riley," greeted Chad without enthusiasm, "to what do we owe the pleasure?"

"I need a few minutes of your time."

Chad's shoulders slumped and he walked to the coat rack to reach for his coat. "The break room will be fine," said Frank.

"Oh! Of course," replied Chad, relief flooding his face. "Celeste, can you take care of booking that job for me, please?" He headed down the short hall ahead of Frank, and stopped beside a chair at the table, turning to face Frank as he followed him into the room. Frank shut the door behind him.

———————

A half hour later, Frank walked into the ME office and found Bruce in the lab. He waited while the tech finished what he was working on and turned towards the Detective.

"Hi Bruce, did you find any finger prints on the box of arsenic we took out of the Roberts' garage?

"Let me see," he said, stripping off the plastic gloves he was wearing and going over to a stack of files. He flipped one open and read the contents. "Yes," he said, looking up at Frank, "but there were no hits. It was a partial."

"Nothing unusual?"

"The partial was a smudge, some kind of varnish on the box." He shrugged his shoulders. "Don't know if that means anything." Frank nodded, rubbing a hand over his chin.

"Find anything interesting in the trash from the Cassin apartment?"

"Not really, just a Chinese take out container, normal stuff. Apparently Ms. Cassin has allergies, because we found three empty bottles of eye drops in the trash in the kitchen and bathroom."

"Any hits on the prints on the take out container?"

"No, I'm sorry, I don't seem to be able to help you much on this one, "the young man said apologetically.

"Don't be so sure," Frank smiled. "I'll get back to you.

―――――――――

Frank was waiting at the apartment when Michelle drove up with Chris in his truck. Chris helped her out of the truck, and had his arm around a very pale Michelle, who was focused on walking carefully to the door. Neither of them noticed him step around the corner until they were almost at the door.

"Detective Riley," she gasped. "Did you have more questions?" She leaned precariously against Chris.

"Can we go inside first?" Chris interjected. "I think she needs to sit down." He shot Frank a look that was a mixture of concern and irritation.

"She can sit in the back of the squad car," Frank answered as Rayburn pulled up behind Chris' truck. "Michelle Cassin, you are under arrest for the murder of Stephanie Devers."

"That's crazy!" shouted Chris.

"Someone tried to kill me, you idiot!" she screeched as Rayburn cuffed her and moved her towards the car. Frank could hear him reading her rights to her as he turned to a dumb struck Chris.

"This is a mistake," Chris protested. "What are you doing? Someone tried to poison Michelle!"

"I'll explain it all at the station," he said with patience.

"Am I under arrest?" asked Chris, shock showing as his mouth gaped.

"No," said Frank. "But I do have some questions for you." He studied the younger man, who was intently staring at the vehicle, with Michelle sitting in the back seat. "Why don't you come with me?" he said gently.

Chapter 48

Frank watched as Chris walked out the door to his truck. He felt sorry for the apparently unwitting participant in Michelle's scheme. He turned and walked to the Captain's office, where he pulled up a chair without waiting to be asked.

"I take it you are here to fill me in on the latest arrest?"queried the Captain, settling back in his chair, his hands clasped over his stomach.

"Yes," said Frank, plopping down heavily. "Get comfortable, this will take awhile."

"Snagging two assumed murderers in one case is worth a little of my time." He put his feet up on the desk and tipped his chair back. "Impress me." His eyes narrowed in anticipation.

"We have a solid case against Nina Roberts for the murder of Ginger Snapper." Frank put a file in the middle of the desk. The Captain didn't move. "Nina confessed to the murder. Motive is tight – she held a grudge against Ginger for over a decade. Nina blamed Ginger for keeping Nina's daughter, Justine, away from her. Frank shivered. "It was cold blooded, premeditated murder, and she is one wicked woman. I am going to make it stick," he said, his jaw set with determination.

The Captain leaned forward and picked up the file. He briefly scanned the contents, then nodded with satisfaction, and set it down. His eyes were expectant as he gestured for Frank to continue.

"What about the second murder and attempted murder?" He leaned forward across his desk now, intent on the answer.

"Michelle killed Stephanie." He let that statement stand alone for a minute as he noted, with some small satisfaction, a glimmer of surprise in the Captain's eyes. "I had some suspicions, but when she said she heard Chad and Nina arguing, I knew she was lying."

"Didn't you already have Nina in custody?" His brows were knitted in concentration.

"Yes, but Stephanie didn't know that because she hadn't been to work. She was already feeling ill, and planned to set up both Chad and Nina."

"Go on," said the Captain after a brief pause.

"We took a closer look at the arsenic used to kill Stephanie. There was only one smudged print on the box of arsenic in the garage.

By the time Bruce processed it, Nina's prints were in the data base and should have shown up, but they didn't. I went back to question Chad about where he got the box of arsenic. He told me he didn't; he assumed Nina picked it up." The Captain opened his mouth to speak, then closed it and sat still a little longer.

"So who got the arsenic?"he finally asked.

"Michelle," Frank said simply. It had taken him awhile to figure the details out, and he was giving the Captain a chance to digest the information a bite at a time. The Captain processed this information while Frank waited.

"How did Michelle buy it? I thought it was harder to get these days."

"She didn't. Arsenic is used in wood working in the curing, because it deters wood eating insects. Michelle's boyfriend, Chris, owns a cabinet making business, so she just went in and helped herself. My guess is, she used gloves so she would not leave prints, but she didn't notice her boyfriends partial print in the varnish stain on the box."

"Is Chris an accessory, then?" asked the Captain. "I'm a little confused."

"No," Frank shook his head, "the poor guy is devastated. He liked Michelle and had no idea what she was really like." Frank glanced out the door, where Chris had walked a few minutes ago. "He voluntarily gave his prints so we could check them against the partial on the box. I think he was half hoping it would prove they weren't his, and she was innocent."

"So, she took some arsenic out and put it in a drink for Stephanie, then planted the box at the Roberts' house?" He looked at Frank for affirmation, and got it. "But, who poisoned Michelle?" The Captain shook his head. "This doesn't make sense!"

"She poisoned herself." Frank let that hang in the air while the Captain processed the information he had just dropped. The man blinked several times before Frank continued.

"Why would she do that?" The Captain said, with shock on his features.

"She didn't know Nina had been arrested for Ginger's murder. She set them up to look guilty for Stephanie, and tried to make it look like they had poisoned her too."

"How in the hell did she do that?"

"Eye drops."

"What are you talking about! Everyone uses eye drops and nobody gets poisoned! "

"If you use them in your eyes, they are fine. But if you ingest them, they are not." Frank shifted forward to face the Captain more closely. "We checked the trash and found no traces of tetrahydrozoline in the Chinese takeout container in Michelle's kitchen garbage. But, Michelle said she got sick after eating the take out Nina gave her. It just didn't fit"

"What is tetrahydrozoline?" asked the Captain.

"It is a chemical in eye drops that constriction of blood vessels, so it works well in the eyes. Ingested, however, it causes seizures, light headedness, and vomiting. It can also cause respiratory distress and death, over a period of time. We found three empty bottles of eye drops in Michelle's trash cans." The Captain stared blankly at him.

"But why would she do that to herself?" asked the Captain. He shook his head and ran his hand over his face.

"She got over zealous. She thought she would just make herself sick, then it would look like Nina and Chad had tried to poison her and failed. She took too much too fast, adding it to her orange juice after having some the previous day in the Chinese food. It sent her into convulsions." He took another sheet of paper out and handed it to the Captain.

"Lab work from the hospital?" The superior officer studied the sheet of paper. "I guess somewhere on here it shows the chemical in her system?"

"Yes. Tying that together with all the bottles of eye drops, that held only her fingerprints, it will be an easy case."

"What about motive?"

"Something she said the first day I met her came back to me. She said 'I could manage this business better myself.' At the time, I thought she was just an unhappy employee."

"Sounds about right," sighed the Captain.

"I asked Chad about that statement the other day. Seems Michelle wanted to be a partner in the business. They declined her offer."

"So, she thought if both owners were in prison, she could just take it over," stated the Captain. "Did she even know about Justine?"

"No, I don't think so. Nina didn't talk about it even to Chad. She didn't want anyone getting suspicious."

"That 's the motive," sighed the Captain. "Money." Both men sat silent for a minute. Finally, the Captain spoke.

"I will never cease to be amazed at people. I remember a case, when I was a rookie, where a man came home and shot his wife dead because he wanted chicken for dinner and she made hamburgers." He scratched his head. "Two people are dead because one held an old grudge and one wanted a business she couldn't have."

Silence hung in the room like a heavy blanket as the two men examined their own thoughts. Frank looked at his Captain and thought he suddenly looked older, his shoulders stooped like a man carrying a weight that was too heavy for too long.

The enormity of death, of lives taken so casually for real or imagined transgressions, made Frank feel like the sun had gone out of the world and blackness was creeping in. He felt cold. He should have been happy to solve the case, but instead, he felt an overwhelming sadness. He bent forward and put his head in his hands, rubbing his eyes.

Suddenly, he thought of Garrett. The young boy was the hope he needed; the bright, happy, innocence of this world, just beginning to grow, and maybe, make a positive impact.

"I don't think I will ever get used to that kind of reasoning, Cap," said Frank softly. The Captain looked at him hard for what seemed like a very long time.

"I hope to hell you never get used to it, Frank," he said quietly.

They stared at each other for several more minutes, until finally Frank nodded in understanding. They did their job, and they did it well, but they never got used to the inhuman things people did to each other.

Frank stood, leaving the files on the Captain's desk for now. They communicated an unspoken good night, and he walked through a quiet squad room.

Outside, he stood, breathing deep of the fresh, clean air, and watched the colors of the sky change into pastels as the sun set. Then he turned and walked slowly to his car.

He had a dinner he needed to make, with a vibrant little boy, a couple who still loved each other after long years together, and a green eyed brunette with a fabulous smile. He really did need to be somewhere where there were normal people for a change.

Made in the USA
Middletown, DE
02 December 2020